"Business as Usual"

By E. Hughes

"Business as Usual"

Love-Love Publishing

ISBN-10: 0985201509
ISBN-13: 978-0985201500

E. Hughes

Other novels by this author:

Disappear, Love by E. Hughes
Infatuation by E. Hughes

I've had the pleasure of spending years of my life
doing what I love because of you...
Thank you for the feedback and well wishes.

"Business as Usual"

4

CHAPTER 1

"Pack your suitcases, we're going to China."

I blinked, and glared through a crack in the door at the imposing figure on the other side before pulling it open, finally allowing my father to walk in. He was fully dressed in one of his expensive business suits, hands clasped tidily behind his back as he strolled into my apartment like it was two in the afternoon. He wore an early morning scowl on his face. The wrinkles creasing his bloodshot eyes revealed an overtired business man. What he needed was a hot shower, a warm bed, and a good night's sleep and not a trip to his daughter's apartment just before the crack of dawn.

"Dad… it's five-o-clock in the morning, I haven't even brushed my teeth," I groaned, wiping sleep from my eyes.

He looked around, inspecting the living room. A stack of files and an open laptop sat on the table next to a cup of cold coffee and a half-eaten bagel. I fell asleep on the couch hours earlier working on a report for the Gold Dust Hotel, one of my father's numerous companies. I was Vice President of Executive Financing at two of our branches, one in Chicago, the other in Atlantic City. I closed the door behind him, securing the lock to my upscale downtown Chicago condo. The high rise building I lived in sat on Michigan Avenue with a view of the city's beautiful skyline and lake.

I walked to the open kitchen and gazed out at my father as he sat on the couch with a grim expression on his face.

"Daddy, can I get you something to drink?" I grabbed a glass from the cabinet. "I can warm some milk for you."

"Thank you, but no," he answered sternly, lifting one of my reports from the table.

"Are these the Vegas projections?"

"Yes, Dad."

"You don't have a graph or a chart to go with these numbers?"

I turned, gazing incredulously at the man. *At 5:30 in the morning?*

"Dad?" I sighed… "If you don't mind, I'd like to finish my report before you start in on it. I fell asleep. But rest assured, I'll have it done before the meeting."

"As long as it's not the final draft…" he frowned.

There was no pleasing him.

Dad worriedly wiped a hand across his bald head. He was tall, dark, and muscular, with the countenance of a drill sergeant, direct and plain spoken unlike the typical smooth-talking billionaire business mogul on the brink of financial ruin. He kept everyone around him on their toes. This particularly early visit was a prime example.

"I know you're tired," he started.

"You have no idea."

I drank my milk then washed and dried the glass by hand before returning it to the shelf.

"*Wo men qu zhong guo wei shenme?*" I asked.

"Sounds like your Mandarin is improving. It'll come in handy when you get to China."

"My intonations need a bit of work. Daddy, why can't I give my report by video conference? We've done it a million times..." I pleaded. I tossed the towel on the sink and skipped to the living room, a look of hope radiating from my eyes. "*Danny'll be here this weekend,*" I beamed, parking my rear on the arm of the sofa.

Daddy scoffed at the mention of Danny's name. No one was good enough for his only daughter *especially* a working class man like Danny who was employed as a registered nurse. I was supposed to marry well. With a proud grin on his face, father rose from his seat on the sofa and strode toward me with outstretched arms. At first, I thought he was offering *me* a hug, but as it turns out, he was the one who needed it. Dad took a step back and gazed at my face, hands resting on my shoulders. "You still have those big beautiful dark eyes," he smiled.

I shrugged his hands away, suddenly uncomfortable. Daddy was hiding something. He had the same look on his face just before he told me my dog died when I was eight years old.

"Elizabeth, I need you more than ever right now. This whole meeting is riding on you."

"Are we in some kind of trouble?"

"We'll find out soon enough." His lips were flat and firm, his jaw tensing as he awaited my response.

"Of course I'll go. I just need a little time to get dressed," I sighed. "What time is our flight?"

Dad grinned from ear to ear. He always got his way. Mother never let me forget how much my father wanted a son. I spent my entire life trying to please him, trying to measure up to what he wanted in a male heir. If that meant taking a flight to China before dawn, then so be it.

Dad shrugged and sat on the sofa again, flipping through the pages of my unfinished report. "Eleven tonight," he answered.

I put my hands on my hips, frowning.

"Why did you wake me up so early? I'm so tired… I feel like a zombie," I yawned.

"We're going to Vegas for the meeting. Afterwards, you'll need a couple hours rest, then we'll head over to the airport for your flight to China. The meeting's at 9 AM so you best get ready so we can stay on schedule. We'll take the private jet."

I pouted as I dragged my tired body upstairs. I wore my thick white socks scrunched down to my ankles, an oversized t-shirt, and my hair pulled into a sloppy ponytail. All I wanted was to sit in my apartment and work on my report with a cup of warm coffee and some music. But, *nooo* he just had to drag me across the country for a stupid two hour meeting.

Dad turned the television on and watched the stock market news while I showered and got dressed. I chose a power suit. A long black pencil skirt and matching blazer that framed my 5'6" figure. I pulled my hair into a sophisticated up-do and put a pair of diamond tear drop earrings in my ears. When I was done, I examined myself in the mirror. I wore a shade of crimson lipstick, an homage to the "power" women of the nineties. The color contrasted against my smooth complexion and dramatic "Elizabeth Taylor" eyebrows, as my dad used to call them.

I packed only a few accessories, business suits for work, and a couple of dresses for the evening into my suitcase. It was Wednesday. With Danny coming for the weekend, my trip to Vegas as well as China would be short and sweet.

I was just about finished packing for my trip when I heard the television. The volume had been turned up loud. I looked over the balcony from my bedroom at father. He sat on the edge of the sofa, remote control in hand, gazing at the screen. Then I heard his name.

"Byron Energy's stock is holding steady after a series of lows at the start of the New year..." the reporter said. *"Recovery has been slow for the energy giant after scandals rocked the company's CEO, Eugene Byron a little over two years ago..."*

Dad tapped his foot on the floor and rubbed his upper thigh. I hated seeing him like this. For a very rich man, Daddy was almost broke. And he was scared. After a vicious Wall Street rumor nearly destroyed his anchor company, Byron Energy, daddy used all of his personal assets to buy millions of shares in order to keep Victor Hampton, the bitter old executive fueling the rumors from taking a controlling share. Victor had designs on dismantling Byron Energy…if he could get his hands on it.

Victor claimed Byron Energy was hiding a mountain of "debt" from investors and was in so much trouble that it was soon to be acquired by AmeriAsia, an overseas land developer. Ironically, the same investor Daddy and I were going to see in Vegas about the budget for the Gold Dust Hotel. He was Daddy's longtime friend. We spent the weekend with the AmeriAsia investors at Daddy's cabin two months ago. It was at my father's insistence that I learn to speak Chinese to accommodate his friend and son, both of whom spoke fluent English. I didn't understand why at the time, but it all was starting to make sense now.

The Vegas deal meant everything to my father as he struggled to rebuild the corporation and his good name. And I would do anything to help him.

CHAPTER 2

Despite an interior the Queen of England would envy, the private plane to Vegas was the ride from hell! I could barely steady my laptop as the turbulent flight shook the entire cabin for almost an hour. When I started to feel the rumblings of an upset stomach, a flight attendant who seconds earlier had been thrown aside as she traveled from one end of the plane to the other, offered Dramamine. I declined. I had work to do and couldn't risk falling asleep. Not that it was possible anyway.

Dad reclined on a sofa chair a few seats ahead and chatted nonstop with two of his assistants about company business. I managed to finish my report nonetheless. I had ten minutes of free time between landing and boarding the limo that awaited us. Without time to freshen up, Dad ordered the driver to the hotel, so I could put my suitcases away, then the Concord Business Center where my father's accounting team and the AmeriAsia investors awaited us.

The facility was a consortium of offices in a mall that included travel by escalator up to various businesses and conference rooms.

"Where are we going?"

"We're going up to the fourth level," Dad said. "To the *Honeymooners* conference room."

I followed him to the escalator and climbed on thinking how weird that sounded. I wondered if Danny was there waiting to surprise me with a marriage proposal and if Dad was in on the secret. My heart fluttered. For the past two years, Danny and I had been in an on and off relationship. He lived in Florida and could only visit a few times a year for a few weeks at a time because of his schedule at the hospital some days working twelve-hour shifts accruing enough flex time to spend a few weeks at my house in San Diego. Our relationship had been gradual. It was only a matter of time before I moved to Florida or Danny moved to California so we could be together.

I chewed on the idea until Dad and I reached the first floor. As I started toward the escalator leading up to the next level, Dad stopped and waved for his assistants to continue on without us.

"Elizabeth, I need to ask you something."

"What is it, Daddy?" I answered, feeling a bit worried. He looked like he was ready to faint.

"A long time ago you told me you would do anything to help me. Is that still true?"

"Of course it's still true! Why would you ask me that? Is something wrong?"

"No," Dad said, "I just want you to know how much I love you."

I wanted to wrap my arms around him. He looked so serious.

"You're not dying are you?"

Dad laughed and shook his head. "Nothing that tragic. Honey, I have something to tell you," he started.

I chewed my bottom lip, waiting for Dad to drop the bombshell he had been keeping from me. I wondered if it had anything to do with my mother or the old Byron Energy scandal, subjects we never discussed.

Suddenly Dad's cell phone rang. Rick and Candace, his two assistants were on the line. They had already made it upstairs. He gave instructions for them to wait at the Cafe for us and told them that we would be attending the meeting alone. When he hung up, he looked at me and said "We'll talk a bit more after the meeting."

Dad left me a befuddled mess as I followed him to the escalator, riding each one to the top until we reached the fourth level.

There were four conference rooms. Ours was at the end of a long narrow tunnel with glass windows overlooking the lower floors.

When Dad and I walked into the *Honeymooners* conference room moments later, to my surprise the only people who showed up for the "big" meeting was Mr. Yu and his strikingly handsome son, Ethan Yu, whose cute face was the first thing I saw when I walked in the door. I let out a little sigh. Both were investors from AmeriAsia, the land developers from China. I wondered where the rest of Dad's staff was and why members from our accounting teams hadn't shown up. The room seemed eerily quiet and tense. I'd known Ethan since I was a kid. It came as no surprise to me that he would grow up to become an even shrewder businessman than his father. We'd spent an inordinate amount of time alone at the weekend retreat while Daddy and Mr. Yu fished and went bird watching. The two men left us at the cabin for hours while they played golf. We had gotten somewhat close, enveloped by a comfortable silence that concealed a slightly muted attraction.

"Nǐ hǎo, Yu Xiān-Shēng *(Hello, Mr. Yu),*" I said, greeting the father as I entered. "Nǐ hǎo *(Hello), Wo hēn Gao-Xing zie jian Nǐn, (Very happy to see you again),*" I said, addressing Ethan right after.

15

He sat straight up in his chair, fully alert, appraising me as I walked by. I followed his gaze from my legs up to my face. Our eyes connected and I smiled.

With his dark shoulder length hair and chiseled face, Ethan was an attractive man. He looked to be in his early thirties now, not much older than me. Our fathers had a friendship that spanned decades. But in all the years of knowing them, as adults, Ethan and I exchanged very few words at the cabin save for the occasional friendly greeting in passing at events where he made a habit of staring at me from beneath a cloak of dark eye lashes when he thought no one was looking.

I prepped my paperwork for the meeting with Ethan's licentious gaze like warm fingertips roaming sensuously up and down my spine, a far cry from the stubborn boy, who once hit me in the eye with a piece of chalk when I was six years old...

When we were kids the two of us had a mutual hatred of being forced to play together while our fathers talked. Now we were the ones doing all of the talking and our fathers were the ones listening.

"Elizabeth?" Daddy called.

"Y-yes, just a moment, please..."

I erased the heedless, sensual imagery of those fingertips bumbling around in the darkness from my mind and fumbled with the papers in my hand. This was neither the time nor place for the silly girlish fantasies I often lapsed into in the presence of gorgeous men.

I opened my laptop, syncing it with the overhead screen I pulled from the ceiling. A platter left by the Café sat on a serving table. There was orange juice, coffee, tea, bottled water, and soda available to drink, as well as fruit, cheese, bacon and croissants for breakfast. I wondered why Dad dismissed his assistants as they would be the ones to pour the coffee and offer refreshments. They were also responsible for setting up the audio and visual equipment.

Sighing, I poured a cup of coffee and said "Refreshments are available if any of you are thirsty or need something to eat." I gestured toward the platter. The Yu men and my father uttered polite refusals.

I moved to the head of the conference table as a picture of one of my charts appeared on screen. Ethan watched from the corner of his eyes as I passed him by.

"Thank you for coming, gentlemen. I should hope the fact that we inadvertently booked the wedding room, that it's a sign that there will be a marriage of ideas between our respective companies after my presentation today."

Black and white photos of women in various wedding dresses decorated the walls in expensive frames. Mr. Yu and Ethan exchanged bewildered glances.

Dad waved, gesturing for me to continue the presentation.

"Carrying on..." I uttered quietly, hoping the awkward silence permeating the room would eventually dissipate.

I adjusted the position of the screen then proceeded to go over the charts and graphs, which detailed the costs associated with the design for the new Gold Dust Hotel.

"As you can see, the designs for the Gold Dust Las Vegas are a bit elaborate. But we could always scale back and make a few changes to meet my projected budget."

"How will the Gold Dust compete with other Vegas hotels if the designs are not as elaborate?" Ethan asked. "This is, a luxury hotel, right?"

I repressed the desire to roll my eyes. "I believe the hotel can be both cost effective and attractive, provided we scale back unnecessary designs," I answered.

Father slid out of his seat as we continued talking and walked over to the serving table to pour some coffee. He mixed cream and sugar into his mug, his back facing the group.

"However, the designs for the hotel are neither attractive nor cost effective," Mr. Yu replied.

I fished around for a worthy reply. "Then what do you suggest is necessary to get costs under control?" I asked.

"What Mr. Yu is saying, Elizabeth, is that we need something a bit more competitive for the Vegas market. All of which, is a moot point, since Mr. Yu and I have already come to an agreement. Have a seat, honey," my father said, like I needed to sit down.

I folded both arms across my chest, annoyed that he had been keeping this secret from me. "If you already had an agreement then what was the point of this meeting?"

I tried not to show how angry I felt as I stormed over to the conference table and sat next to my father, directly across from Ethan and Mr. Yu.

"I have good news. Mr. Yu, has agreed to invest in the Gold Dust Las Vegas as an equal partner on the condition that Ethan, who is an architect, redesigns the hotel and oversees its construction. I felt, since you already worked so hard on the previous project, overseeing its budget, that we should at least hear you out."

"So where do we go from here?" I asked, ignoring the fact that Dad allowed me to work on the budget knowing they had no intention of approving the project.

"The good news, Elizabeth, is that we would like you to oversee the budget on the new project. So nothing has changed in that regard except that you will be working closely with Ethan to get this done. With Mr. Yu's help, we've secured the funds we needed to complete this massive undertaking. We expect this to be one of the grandest hotels in Vegas history."

"Congratulations," I answered coldly, ignoring Ethan's pensive stare as he drummed the end of his pen on the table absently.

"There's more…" father continued. "I'm not sure how you'll feel about this Elizabeth, but I really need your help."

Finally, the truth was coming out. I wondered what type of imposition would follow next. "What is it?"

"Now that AmeriAsia, of which, Ethan is part owner, has a controlling interest in the Gold Dust Hotel, the government will adjust his Visa status. Unfortunately, the adjustment will bar Ethan from working and traveling to the U.S. His current Visa gives him employee status, it does not grant him permission to visit the States as a business owner, which is what he will become after the agreement has been signed. Unfortunately, Mr. Yu's investment depends entirely on Ethan overseeing the project."

"In other words, the deal is off if Ethan can't oversee the project here in the States. What can we do to help?"

I waited for father to continue, as I was obviously missing the point. All eyes in the room were on me.

"A green card would allow Ethan to live in the United States for ten years, with the opportunity to apply for permanent residency in five. We've spoken to various attorneys about obtaining a new Visa status or immediate residency for Ethan, and unfortunately, all avenues have been exhausted. It could take years and we don't have a lot of time. However, there is one other option that we haven't discussed with our attorneys... with good reason. If Ethan were to marry he could not only apply for a green card right away, but also permanent residency after three years."

Daddy sat his briefcase on the table, took some documents out, and sat one before me, Mr. Yu, and Ethan.

I looked at the document, which read

"Business as Usual"

Prenuptial Agreement:

*This agreement made in triplicate this
12th day of February, 2012*

Parties:

*Ethan 'Xiaoming Yu
(Of the city of Las Vegas in the State of Nevada)*

and

*Elizabeth Byron
(Of the city of San Diego in the State of California, & the
city of Chicago, in the State of Illinois)*

This prenuptial Agreement is made between Ethan 'Xiaoming Yu' thereinafter referred to as "Mr. Yu" and Elizabeth Byron, thereinafter referred to as "Ms. Byron", who are contemplating marriage to each other...'

I read the line *who are contemplating marriage to each other*' twice. When had I contemplated marriage to anyone other than Danny?

"What in the hell is this?" I asked, unleashing the fury building within me ever since my father revealed that he and Mr. Yu had already worked out an agreement.

"I am *not* to be bartered as a part of some business deal!" I shrieked. "How dare you!" I was out of my seat, pointing my finger accusingly at my father's face. Dad had seen me angry before, but that anger had never been directed at him. He looked shocked, not quite expecting my reaction. Realizing that I was on the brink of losing control I rescinded the invectives rolling to the tip of my tongue and waited for my father to speak.

"You have two minutes then I am out of here!"

Dad was on his feet in seconds, hands on my shoulders as if to keep me from leaving the room.

"I'm sorry, Elizabeth, I had no idea this would upset you so much."

"How could this not upset me? You lied to get me to come to Vegas when you already worked something out with Mr. Yu. Then you present me with some prenuptial agreement for Ethan Yu? Are you mad? Have you lost your *mind?*"

Who did my father think he was, planning my life in such a manner and under such shady conditions!

"You have no right to ask this of me. I'm not marrying *him or anybody else!*" I scoffed. I felt Ethan's now piercing gaze on my back as I glared at father.

"Perhaps, we should give the two of you a moment," Mr. Yu suggested with a disappointed look on his face.

The situation was my father's fault. Mr. Yu and Ethan discussed their end of the deal at length, perhaps weeks in advance of coming to Vegas. They were on the same page, but my father and I were not. I felt bad about my choice of words and for flat out refusing in the manner I did. I realized how mortified the two men must have been. Though neither could have been more mortified than I felt when my father and Mr. Yu finally revealed their hair-brained scheme.

"I apologize for my behavior, Mr. Yu. It's just that, this is a bit unexpected. Not to mention illegal." I ignored Ethan and focused on his father, who over the years had been so kind to me.
"I can make my investments in China or some other company," Ethan snapped, the color draining from his face. "I don't need this."
He gathered the documents he had been given from the table, dropping some of them on the floor

E. Hughes

as he stalked out with Mr. Yu chasing his haughty son out the door. Finally, my father and I were alone.

"How could you?" I asked.

"I'm sorry I lied, baby. But I knew you wouldn't come if I told you."

"What about Danny? What about the fact that you are asking me to commit a crime?"

"I would never impose on you if it wasn't absolutely necessary, sweetie. I don't feel good about this," he said, lowering his head. "But I wouldn't ask if Ethan wasn't a good guy. I'm not asking you to consummate the marriage."

"Dad!"

I started to storm out, but Dad lifted a hand, gesturing for me to stay. "Lizzie, come on. You said you would do anything for me. I've given you everything you could ever ask for and I ask you to do one thing for me, and you can't help me out? And it's not like an arranged marriage is really a crime."

I folded both of my arms. "Semantics. And the guilt trip is *not* working."

"Three years, that's all I ask. Ethan is a respectful young man, his father and I are good friends, and we know the two of you will get along. I know you love Danny. But... he's not right for you, honey."

25

"And Ethan is?"

I turned away from my father, sighing.

"You promised you would do anything for me, Elizabeth. I dedicated my entire life to raising you, putting you through college, and helping you buy your condo. When have I asked for anything in return?"

"I never asked for any of those things!" I countered.

"When your mother walked out," he said, voice lowering, "who stayed behind to pick up the pieces? When you were devastated, I was there for you," father accused.

How long was he going to use that against me? Of course Dad was right. He was there for me, through thick and thin, rain hail sleet or snow. But I couldn't help but wonder… if he was willing to break laws to build his hotel, would he be willing to engage in illegal maneuvers for Byron Energy? Were the rumors true? I didn't want to know.

"I'm a proud man," my father said. "Please, Lizzie. Don't make me ask again."

And that was his plea. *Don't make him ask again.* From the sound of his voice I knew the hotel wasn't the only thing on the line. "What are you so afraid of?" I asked.

Dad sighed, and his jaws tensed as he shoved his hands into his pockets and looked down. "Please, honey? You're the only person in the world I can turn to right now. I need you, sweetie."

My heart broke when I looked into Daddy's eyes. The marriage would be a piece of paper, legal and binding like numerous contracts I signed throughout the week. Then it would be over. Ethan was in on the plan so nothing would really change, except marrying Danny would happen later than I originally planned.

"And how long would I have to stay married to him?" I begrudgingly asked.

"Three years and that's it, honey."

Dad gathered the prenuptial agreement from the table and held it before me.

"Ethan already signed."

Dad pointed at Ethan's signature. Was this really happening? Would I go through with something so shady? Would my father ask me to do something like this if he weren't in serious trouble?

I wanted to ask him about his problems again, but I knew he would never tell me. Dad would not want me to worry about him. All I had to do was get married and pretend to be in love for three years to help my father with a multi-billion dollar deal.

Thinking about it further, what was in it for Mr. Yu and his son? Like Ethan said, there were other businesses he could easily invest in and monitor from China. Something was going on and I was determined to get to the bottom of it. Just as Daddy's stock was beginning to recover, AmeriAsia was on the scene again. The timing was suspect and Daddy was nervous.

"Fine, Daddy... I'll do it. But hell or high water, if this thing lasts more than three and a half years, I'm done. Contract or not."

Marrying Ethan would get me that much closer to the truth. It was a sacrifice worth making for a man who had endured so much over the past few years. Lies, treachery, and hostile takeovers...he'd been through it all and was still standing. I was certain he had a plan and would let me in on it later, I just had to dig up the evidence he needed when the time was right.

In a fit of excitement Dad pulled me into a bear hug, sweeping me off of my feet as he spun me around.

"Thank you, Lizzie! You won't regret this, I promise baby. I know this is a bit of a sacrifice, but on the plus side, a few perks comes with the arrangement."

Dad set me back on my feet and flipped through the pages of the contract.

"You get $500,000 for every year that you're married. You get an additional $500,000 for every male child that results from the union, $250,000 for each female child."

"Dad! You said no one is expecting us to consummate this marriage. It's not real, remember?"

"Right, but just in case the two of you…"

"It's not going to happen!" I snapped. "I'm in love with Daniel, got it?"

"This business with Daniel Williams is finished," said father, tersely. "He's a threat."

"The only threat is you!" I snapped. "Just when I thought we were getting closer, you pull this rabbit out of your hat."

"I'm prepared to do what I must to protect you, Elizabeth. And if that means playing hardball to keep Daniel out of the picture then so be it. The Byron name, our livelihood, and your freedom is on the line. I need you to understand that."

"Leave him alone, Dad. He didn't do anything to any of us. Stay away from Danny or the deal's off, I mean it."

"Okay…okay," Dad said, backing off. "Let's get this document signed and the two of you can head over to the chapel and make it legal."

"Wait, you don't expect us to get married today?"

"Why else would we have the meeting in Vegas? Quickie weddings!" Dad exclaimed, rushing toward the door. "You can do it the day after tomorrow. Okay?" He gestured for Mr. Yu and Ethan to come back inside, waving them in. The men had been waiting in the corridor for me and Dad to finish our private chat.

"I have terrific news... Elizabeth has agreed to marry Ethan," Dad announced.

Mr. Yu broke into a smile. "Welcome to the Yu family, Elizabeth," he said, taking me by the hands.

"Thank you, Mr. Yu. Again, I apologize for my reaction, earlier."

"You have no one to blame... *but your father*," he winked. "I'm sure you and Ethan will get along just fine."

I nearly forgot about the man at the center of our rift. Ethan, who had come in behind his father moments earlier, shrugged then sat at the conference table, completely unruffled, leg folded across his lap. He fished around his pocket for a cigar, which he proceeded to smoke in the room, despite the "No-Smoking" sign on the wall.

While I stood there wondering why Ethan would be willing to go through with the farce that was to be our marriage, father called Rick, his assistant, and told him to bring a notary signing Agent to the conference room. Thankfully, the Concord had a notary office for the various business deals taking place at the mall.

"It's 1:25 and I have a plan to catch," Mr. Yu said, gathering documents and stuffing them into his briefcase.

I wondered why he wasn't staying for my fake wedding to his son.

"You're leaving?" I asked.

Mr. Yu smiled.

"When a young couple in love runs away to elope in Las Vegas, their parents are not usually part of the process."

If only we were a young couple in love! I thought.

Rick arrived with a notary agent twenty minutes later, long enough for my father and Mr. Yu to witness my signing of the document. But not before my father left us with a bit of advice. And then we were alone.

"You are officially on vacation, effective immediately," my father said. "Ethan booked a trip...a honeymoon of course, for appearances sake. As far as I know, you'll be taking the eleven o' clock flight to China with Ethan tonight. I understand a second wedding is to take place in Guangzhou."

"I changed my mind about going to China. We'll go when Elizabeth is ready. I have something else in mind for our honeymoon," Ethan said.

"Would have been nice if you shared those arrangements with me," I said. "I'm a part of this too."

Ethan shrugged and puffed his cigar like he didn't have a care in the world, which really pissed me off. The sanctity of marriage clearly meant nothing to him, whereas I was completely torn up about our situation.

"Spend time together like young newlyweds. Trust me, shit will hit the fan when news about your marriage gets out. The media will question the authenticity of your relationship."

"With good reason," I quipped.

"It's not a joke," my father said, looking serious. "I don't want you to get in trouble."

"Yadda yadda yadda, I get it Dad, pretend we're married for real."

"We will be," Ethan said.

"On paper," I shot back. The only man I wanted to be married to 'for real' was Danny.

Ethan and I watched as our fathers left, leaving us alone in the big empty conference room. If this was a business meeting, would I have reservations about being alone with Ethan, working quietly side by side?

Ethan waited until the door was closed then shuffled the neatly coiffed hair style he'd adopted in his father's presence into a mess of hair. He then leaned against the edge of the conference table, sitting down as he knocked our prenuptial agreement and a pile of other documents onto the floor.

What were we supposed to say to each other now that we were getting married? I scraped the documents from the floor and sat them on the table again, anything to avoid looking at him. Suddenly, Ethan perked up like he remembered something important.

"I have something for you," he said, reaching into the interior of his jacket.

I waited, afraid of what he was about to do as he dove into his pocket. Ethan produced a small black ring box and extended it toward me. I shook my head in dismay.

"Really, Ethan… it's not necessary. Please don't," I protested.

"What's wrong?" he replied nonchalantly, popping the box open. I flinched like he offered a pox infected blanket. Ethan smacked his lips derisively and grabbed my hand, gripping it firmly as he pulled me close enough to see what was inside of the box. His lips were a breath away from my face. Suddenly, my heart was in my throat. I was supposed to be looking at the ring, but instead found myself staring ahead at the lines of his chest, showing where the buttons parted at the top of his shirt. I was suddenly acutely aware of his maleness and the all too primitive potential behind it. What was Ethan like outside of the office? *What if I actually started to like him?*

Resenting my errant thoughts I pretended to focus on the ring. "It's really beautiful," I said, biting down an overwhelming desire to cry. I'd been imposed upon in the worst way. My actions or inaction could shape the future of not only our companies, but whether or not Ethan would stay in America.

"Lau po? Shenme shi?"

"Wo mei shi (I'm fine)!" I snapped. "And don't call me wife. I'm not your wife."

The musty smell of Ethan's cigar was stagnant as he blew a cloud of smoke into the air. I gave him an irate look as he extended the ring box again. "Put it on," he said, with a familiarity I resented.

I finally looked at the ring. It was a gorgeous crystal clear rose tinted diamond. "It's beautiful," I said. "But I can't accept it."

"Why not," Ethan asked, gazing fiercely into my eyes.

"It's too generous. A ring this beautiful deserves a real engagement."

The rose colored diamond was extremely rare, and also very expensive. Why would he invest so much in a marriage that wasn't even real? Ethan sighed.

I found myself gazing at the aquarium on the other side of the room, looking at the exotic sea fish swimming around the large saltwater tank. I longed for a life so uncomplicated and simple as trickling noises from the filter filled the room.

Ethan took the ring out of the box and slid it onto my finger. The gesture was too much. "What are you doing?" I demanded, trying to draw my hand away from him.

"The lady doth protest too much, methinks," he smiled, strengthening his grip with a devious grin on his face. "It's just a ring, Elizabeth."

I rolled my eyes. Why'd he have to be so cute?

"We might as well get used to each other" he said. "We'll be sharing our lives for a long time." Ethan leaned close and swept an arm around my waist, drawing my body close to his. I gave him a look like

35

he had lost his mind despite the inexplicable heat emanating between us.

"That's all we'll be sharing, so don't get any ideas!" I huffed.

"I'm not the one with the ideas," he teased, "But now that you mention it…"

Just as I pressed my hand against his chest with enough force to push him away, the door opened and Dad's assistant, Rick walked in. I looked up, almost guiltily, realizing that Ethan was not only still holding me, but had interlocked his fingers with mine.

Ethan stood about 5'10 with medium length dark hair that swept his shoulders. In my heels we were almost the same height. His face showed signs of stubble growing in, and a closer look at his eyes revealed dark circles. He'd been up all night.

. "Oh, sorry to interrupt," Rick said. "Your father told me to grab the audio equipment."

"No problem," I answered smoothly, sliding out of Ethan's grasp. "We'll be done in a minute."

"Cool," Rick answered. "Congratulations on your engagement," he offered.

"Thanks," Ethan replied. "I'm the lucky one with such a pretty wife so thank her."

I hid both of my hands behind my back to keep from wringing his neck! "We're, technically not married yet," I stammered, "but thank you."

Ethan was going to make this difficult. Already, he was so exasperating. Rick left, closing the door behind him with a promise to come back.

"What was that about?" I asked.

"How can people believe we're a couple if we don't interact with each other? You look so alarmed. The glow of love is missing from your eyes."

Ethan was right. If the government caught us he would be deported and I would end up going to jail for immigration fraud. Looking like a real couple was detrimental. How could my own father get me involved in something like this? No doubt he truly believed I could pull it off. My shoulders sagged.

"I see your point," I acquiesced. "But… how can you be so calm? Why aren't you taking this seriously?" Ethan was way too nonchalant about the whole ordeal.

"Why would I be upset about marrying a pretty American girl?"

Despite my Ivy League pedigree and the fact that I was vice president of an upscale hotel chain, the only thing Ethan saw was a pretty girl standing before him. A flash of unabashed desire flickered in his eyes.

"Whatever!"I exclaimed dismissively, rolling my eyes. I suppose we better get this thing started. What are we supposed to do now?"

Ethan grabbed my hand. "You can follow me," he said, pulling me toward the door. "How's that for starters?"

"Where are we going?"

"We'll go get our marriage license, shopping for something to wear then to the jewelry store to pick out wedding bands. We can go to the chapel later tonight. How does that sound?"

Ethan opened the door and the both of us walked out.

It sounds like I'm in a shit load of trouble... I thought.

CHAPTER 3

After leaving the Concord Business Center, Ethan used his cell phone to summon the driver of the sleek, navy blue Maybach 57s he rented to courier us over to the Palazzo, an upscale mall about a mile out from the strip.

En route, he phoned concierge at our hotels and had someone ship his belongings to my room. He then removed his suit jacket and tossed it on the seat while absently rolling up the sleeves of his button down shirt, showing smooth but muscular arms. He spoke with a level of authority in his voice, detailing how he preferred to have his clothing packed, and where to leave them in my room, referring to me as Mrs. Yu. I stayed in a one bedroom penthouse suite at the top of the Luxury Grand Tower Hotel. I waited for him to request a roll-away bed, but no such command was ever made.

The five minute ride to the Shoppes at the Palazzo took an eternity. My mind was in a haze and I felt a headache coming on. When we finally arrived, Ethan climbed out of the vehicle, walked around to the sidewalk, then opened my door. He immediately took my hand, gripping it firmly in his as he pulled me out of the car. He studied me with the air of a man used to being in control.

"Let's walk the rest of the way," he said.

"Why?"

"So people can see us. I want to be seen with you." He grazed the side of my face with his fingers until he was cupping my chin. I resisted the urge to smack his hand away.

The walkway was deserted, save for the tall, muscular, olive-complexioned man exiting a vehicle two cars behind us. He stood on the sidewalk, wire plugged into his ear, arms folded across his chest. Our eyes connected and he gave me a hard look. I averted my gaze and clung to Ethan's hand. What if someone took a picture and Danny saw it? How would I explain it to him? I rethought the gesture and slipped my hand out of Ethan's grasp, only to find him reaching out to grab it again.

I was growing more and more annoyed by the minute. Not only was the situation highly irritating, but the five-inch heels I wore pinched my toes, adding to my misery. "That's fine," I said, feeling a bit like a push over.

We stood on the cobbled walkway outside of Barney's, the warm desert breeze blowing on our faces. The imported palm trees lining Vegas streets for miles on end was the perfect backdrop for my fake relationship.

Ethan's phone rang. We held hands as he spoke Mandarin in a rushed manner to the person on the other line. My ears perked as I wondered who he was talking to after hearing "Byron" float by in the conversation. But Ethan spoke so quickly, I could only comprehend a few words at a time. Was he talking to his father? *Or someone else?* I heard something about "the company" and "dropping stocks." He turned his back, plugging a finger into one ear and lowering his voice so I could not hear. What was the young man plotting and would my father know anything about it? I wondered if this was the reason why my father insisted I learn to speak Mandarin and now, I wish I had practiced the language more often.

When Ethan hung up I said, "There's a dress boutique just down the walk called Maria Bella's. You can buy something at Barney's and I can go there to shop for a dress." He'd like Barney's. It was a high end department store, a good excuse to go separate ways. I needed a moment to clear my head.

"I already have a suit. I bought it a few weeks ago." He shoved both of his hands into his pockets and casually followed me to the store.

How long ago had Ethan, Mr. Yu and my father been planning this?

I felt an overwhelming desire to tell him to get lost as we walked the block and a half to Maria Bella's. I hadn't a moment's peace since I agreed to marry him and could hardly catch my breath. The hand holding, the ring, the shopping and the planning...it was all too much. Ethan walked at a breathtaking pace and was soon leading the way. I studied his lean but muscular physique from behind. It seemed for every step he took, I had to take two to keep up. Deportation had to be imminent. It was the only explanation I could come up with as to why he was in a hurry to marry a woman whom in the past, he'd barely made an effort to talk to.

When we walked into Maria Bella's, one of the sales girls greeted me by name, even though I had only visited a few times. No doubt they remembered the commission they earned from my previous visits. It didn't take long for Adriana, the 60-ish, Italian boutique owner to get wind of my visit. She dutifully met us at the front of the store to personally assist us. I told her what I was looking for and without making a fuss, she went to the back to have a look at her inventory.

I'd forgotten how much I liked the boutique's elegant look and its authentic Victorian styled gold-trimmed furniture. I studied the décor as I sat on a nearby chaise absently gathering a sofa pillow to my chest. Ethan stood with a sales girl at the front of the store, openly admiring a Victorian ivory inlaid gold cabinet. The young woman grinned playfully as they chatted then placed a hand on Ethan's arm. I felt an inexplicable prick of jealousy. Feeling my gaze, he looked up, catching my eye but I quickly turned away, putting the pillow back where I found it.

A few minutes later he joined me and Adriana at the back of the store, much to the manager's surprise.

"Congratulations! I can't believe you are getting married. I haven't seen anything in the papers about it. Is this handsome young man your fiancé?" Adriana teased, peering curiously at Ethan.

"Oh, I'm sorry, this is Ethan Yu..." I replied, ignoring her question.

"Nice to meet you," he answered shoving both of his hands into his pockets. I spied a look of irritation on Ethan's face as we followed Adriana to the other room.

"This is truly a blessed event," the woman chattered. "We can tailor a gown for you if you need it. Are you going to one of the chapels?"

"Yes, we're going to Blue Bird Wedding Temple. Why don't we have a look at some of your new inventory? I'm looking for a cream or white dress. Maybe something with a vintage design... I'm thinking 1930s chic."

I pulled the raven haired Sophia Loren lookalike by the arm as quickly as I could, doing my best to leave Ethan at the front of the store. We were already feeling too much like a couple, even if only on the surface.

"Actually," he interjected, "white is bad luck in Chinese culture...it represents the color of death."

"Then what am I supposed to wear?" I asked.

"Red is lucky," Ethan replied.

It was my fake wedding and I couldn't even get the dress I wanted? What difference did it make if red was lucky?

"Red wedding dresses are quite common actually," Adriana said. She then pointed an accusing finger at Ethan. "Stay here. It's bad luck to see the gown before the wedding."

She pulled me by the arm and escorted me to a room in the back, leaving Ethan to chat with the

44

sales girl at the front of the store again. I sighed, grateful to get away.

"Because of the color, you'll want to avoid a big poufy dress... red can be so overpowering."

Adriana went to the storage room at the back of the store and returned a few minutes later wheeling a clothes rack behind her. Several dresses zipped into beige dry cleaning bags hung from the stand.

"I have a vintage 1930s satin organdie dress with spaghetti straps in a rich vibrant red. It's lengthy though not quite a fishtail design. It has a loose-fitting shape but manages to frame the womanly curves of your body. Your fiancé won't be disappointed, I promise you."

I ignored her last comment as Adriana unzipped a dry cleaning bag, revealing the red satin dress. '*Ethan and I are not in love and never will be*,' I thought. What did it matter if he liked the dress?

Nevertheless, when Adriana revealed the gown I was overjoyed. It was exactly what I wanted only in a different color.

"It's gorgeous!" I exclaimed. "Can I try it on? If it looks as good on me as it does on this hanger, I would love to buy it off the rack if possible?"

"I knew you'd love it. And of course you can buy it off the rack for your special day. It's one of a kind.

If alterations are needed, I have a seamstress who can assist you."

I scurried into the fitting room.

As I slid into the dress I couldn't help but wonder... why did it matter if white was unlucky or the color of death? If anything, we needed a little bad luck as the marriage was *supposed* to fail.

I gazed into the floor length mirror in the cozy little fitting room and loved the way the beautiful satin organdie gown clung to my figure, the way the spaghetti straps slipped down my shoulders, and how long and tall it made me feel. I also loved the way it dipped in the back down to my lower spine, how soft it was against my skin... this dress deserved a man who loved me, not some fake wedding to save a business deal.

I came out of the fitting room and spun around. "I'll take it!"

"Very good," Adriana said. "But you need something for your hair."

A veil wouldn't look right. "Maybe a comb, or a flower?" I suggested.

Adriana chewed the end of her fingernail. "I may have something for you. But it's expensive. I'll have the seamstress make some adjustments to the dress while I look for it, if that is okay with you?"

"Of course," I said.

While Adriana looked for the accessory, a woman of seventy or so years with silver hair came out to do the alterations. I tried not to move as the woman fixed my dress. She even pricked me a few times while complaining about my inability to keep still between probing me with questions about my nuptials.

"How long have you been engaged?"

"Just a few days," I lied. What was I supposed to say? That I'd been engaged for roughly an hour, give or take a few minutes? I winced when the woman pricked me again.

"Sorry!" she exclaimed. "I'm almost done." The woman licked the end of her needle then stabbed at the dress once more.

"I'm not a fool. My daughter eloped when she was seventeen!" the woman huffed. "Shame on you! Young people, breaking your parents' hearts. Aye!" she scoffed. "You can step down now."

I climbed off of the wooden stoop and thanked the poor woman, wondering how she had arrived at such a conclusion. I then walked to the front of the store where, for reasons unknown to me, I found myself looking for Ethan.

I waited by the register and soon, Adriana appeared with a small white box in her hand. Inside, there was a beautiful gold plated comb in the shape of a butterfly fitted with red jewels.

"Are those rubies?" I gasped.

"The comb is very expensive… but worth every penny," she beamed.

Adriana pushed the comb into my hair, pinning it up on the sides. I turned around so I could see how it looked in the mirror.

"See how beautiful it looks against your dark hair?" she smiled.

"It's very beautiful," I said. "I'll take it."

Adriana gave the items to a clerk who took it to a room where she packaged them for me. When the young clerk returned, I gave her my credit card, ready to settle the bill, when the young woman told me Ethan had already taken care of it. The man was too much!

The young clerk carried the box outside to the Maybach, where Ethan waited. I climbed in. We went to the court house directly to buy a marriage license, few words passing between us when others were not around. Though there was a moment, when I looked up and found him gazing at me with through hooded eyes.

CHAPTER 4

"It guess it's official…" Ethan said, a self-congratulatory smirk on his face.

I signed and dated our marriage license then passed the document to the administrator on the other side of the window at the courthouse.

"So it is," I tersely replied. *Just another business deal…* I could back out at any time, but I knew I wouldn't be able to forgive myself for disappointing my father. There were consequences for disappointment, like being written out of the Byron family and out of my father's life.

Ethan's hand rested on the small of my back as the man at the window reviewed the information on the form to ensure everything was in order. Ethan's hand was warm, his fingers tracing a pattern on my spine. Strangely, he didn't seem as unhappy about the arrangement as he should be. In fact, he looked downright jovial.

We left the courthouse and went to the hotel a short time later. There, Ethan's clothes and other personal belongings were waiting for us. Someone had already hung our clothes in the same closet, and placed his shaving kit and other toiletries in the bathroom with mine.

The suite was spacious with a king sized bed, walk-in closet and large picturesque windows with a stunning view of a glitzy Las Vegas skyline. I waited until Ethan was properly settled in the other room as I weighed telling Danny about my marriage of convenience.

Daniel was beautiful, almost fairy-like with his long wavy golden hair that he'd practically been growing since birth, while Ethan was action star handsome, tall, athletic, and brooding. He was also an avid mountain climber with a physicality that Daniel lacked.

I got my cell phone out and called Danny. He answered on the first ring. I was going to tell him everything until I heard his soft-spoken voice on the line. Could I really break his heart? How do you tell the man you love you're about to marry someone else?

"If it isn't my second most favorite girl in the world..."

There was a patient in the room...a little girl. I could hear her giggles in the background. Danny definitely had a way with the ladies.

"*Daniel...hi,*" I said, as I steadied my shaking hands.

I wanted to kick myself for being so spineless. I hated disappointing people, even when my own happiness was at stake, as I embarked on the journey of a loveless marriage. Most people divorced to get out, and here I was, marrying in.

"Hey, babe. It's good to hear your voice. "What's good?"

"Not much," I answered dryly. "I'm on the road."

"Another amazing trip? That's *cool...*" said a perpetually happy, Danny. "Where are you and when are you coming back? I can't wait to see you, baby."

"Are you with a patient?"

"Just finishing up!"

"Good."

"You sound weird. What's wrong?" he asked, concern edging his voice.

"Are you alone?"

"I am now." His voice dropped. I heard a door close in the background, then Daniel's soothing tone. "Spit it out, spider. What's going on?"

"You have to cancel your flight to San Diego."

"Whoa, what happened? You okay?"

"I'm fine," I answered solemnly.

"That makes one of us. So what brought this on?" He sounded sad and confused.

"Work," I answered quietly…*guiltily*.

The last thing in the world I wanted to do was involve Danny in my family's lies, or worse, make him a target of my father's threats. One phone call from Eugene and Daniel would be out of a job, an apartment, or worse, until he was out of my life.

"You're blowing me off and I want to know why," he demanded. "Is it your father again?"

I wasn't a good liar. In fact, I was a terrible liar. But I tried anyway…an excuse until I could think of a way of breaking up with him without breaking his heart.

"It's not Eugene," I muttered, chewing the end of my fingernails. "Remember the hotel I told you about?"

"The one in Vegas?" he asked, sounding suspicious. I tried to sound cool.

"Yeah. I'll be working on the budget until we break ground. We have an investor here from China, a land developer who will be working on the blueprint. I've been tasked with keeping the project on budget. He's here for a short time so my life pretty much revolves around his schedule. We'll be joined at the hip for weeks. We're spending so much time together we're one step away from his and her towels," I sputtered, an ill-attempt at humor and the truth.

"If I didn't know better, I'd think he was trying to steal my girl!" Danny answered, sounding justifiably worried. "Look, I have to go. Gotta make rounds," he said.

"Don't let me keep you," I replied, coiling my fingers in and out of the phone cord.

"Call me tomorrow, I love you…"

Danny's words hung in the air.

A short time after we hung up, I found solace in the mini-bar, drowning my woes away with little bottles of vodka as I kicked my shoes off and peeled out of my clothes, leaving a trail of undergarments in my wake. Then I saw it…a small black briefcase. It sat open on the nightstand next to the bed. Unable to resist, I peeked inside. There was a document on top written in Chinese, but the logo of my father's company in the right hand corner was unmistakable. I heard a noise, snapped the briefcase closed, and disappeared into the bathroom, heart thumping wildly in my chest.

I peeked through a crack in the door as Ethan bumbled around in the bedroom, retrieving the briefcase. He pressed a button to open it then checked the contents suspiciously before closing it again. He then returned to the living room where he worked on his laptop and talked nonstop on the phone in rapid-fire Chinese.

I closed the door and ran a bath, thinking about the mysterious documents while trying to remember if I had eaten anything as a flush of heat raced through my body and my stomach churned. I wasn't that worried. My days as a sorority girl had taught me I could consume almost a deadly amount of liquor, even on an empty stomach. But still, the mini-bottles of liquor were slowly taking its toll.

I raked my hands through loosened strands of hair and took a deep breath as I recounted the events of the day like a post traumatic stress victim, ranting obscenities at my father and Ethan in my head over and over again, saying all the things I wish I'd said at the meeting until some of the anxiety boiling inside of me had been released. With my hair hastily pushed into a bun at the back of my head I wiped a bead of sweat from my brow. It was hot. I had shut the air conditioning down when we left our luggage at the hotel just before the meeting. So I turned the bathwater off, covered up in a silk black robe, and marched out of the bedroom to turn it back on.

Sweltering desert heat filled the penthouse like helium filling a latex balloon. Ethan paced the living room and unfastened his tie while smoothing damp hair away where it clung to the side of his face. The underarms of his shirt were soaked and his chest glistened. There was something about the sight of a virile young man dripping with sweat that made my limbs weak. I turned the control on the air conditioner, setting the temperature to forty-five degrees.

"It's hot in here," he complained, looking up at me for the first time. Ethan's eyes climbed my legs up to the thigh length silk black robe.

"The air conditioning's on. Can I get you something to drink?"

"sh-sure," he stammered, walking toward me with his shirt half buttoned.

I turned on my heels and walked to the bar with a grin on my face. I could feel the heat of his gaze on my back as he followed me across the room. I grabbed two glasses and a bucket of ice and poured us a glass of Patron. I passed the drink to Ethan. He placed the glass to his lips, taking a sip.

"Ready for tonight?" he asked, gazing intently into my eyes. I wasn't sure if he was talking about the wedding or whatever he was expecting to happen after it.

"Oh, as ready as I can be, considering the circumstances."

I slid an ice cube across my neck, rubbing it up and down until water melted into my cleavage. He followed the drip with his eyes then took another sip of liquor as if to vanquish the image from his thoughts. "

"What about you?"

Ethan shrugged. "What about me?"

"Aren't you nervous?"

"There's nothing to feel nervous about."

"How can you say that? It's not like you wanted to marry me or I wanted to marry you."

Ethan frowned. "Is the idea of being married to me that disgusting to you?"

"It's not you," I stammered. "I have a boyfriend. What about you? Do you have a girlfriend back home in China?"

Ethan sat his glass on the counter then took mine from out of my hand, his face contorted in anger. "You realize you have to give him up, right?"

"I don't have to do anything," I said, lifting my chin to give him a defiant look.

Even though I'd already made the decision to break things off with Danny, I wasn't going to let

Ethan think he could bully me or control my life. I did it to protect the man I loved. Our breakup had nothing to do with him.

"The only reason I'm marrying you is because I don't want to disappoint my father."

I backed into the bar as Ethan settled my drink on the countertop. He tried to look away before I noticed the jealous gleam in his eyes.

"And part of keeping that promise is acting like a married woman. I don't care about your love life, Elizabeth, but I won't be humiliated. Understand?"

"I already have a father, Ethan. I don't need two!" Jealous? *Really*? The nerve!

I left Ethan at the bar but could feel his swift angry strides at the heels of my feet as I stormed to the bedroom. He grabbed the doorknob before I could reach it, pulling the door closed.

"I'm not your father, Elizabeth... but I *will be* your husband. Try not to forget it," he huffed, parking his hands on his hips like an angry woman.

"You won't be anything if I change my mind," I snapped, lifting my chin defiantly.

Was he serious? We hadn't even said our vows and he was already butting into my private affairs. The marriage was temporary and so was my separation from Daniel. In the past, I had been the selfless one in my family, always trying to make everyone happy whereas Ethan was just a spoiled billionaire brat used to getting his way. He pushed the door open and I marched inside without another word, slamming it closed. Then I laid on the king-sized bed and cried as I contemplated backing out of the contract over and over again. But as much as my father loved me, he wasn't a forgiving man... especially when it came to people not keeping their word. I'd seen the way he treated my mother when she went against his wishes. I had a choice to make. I could tell my father to go to hell, and lose the only family I had, or endure the loveless three year marriage I committed to. Whatever I decided, I had to be strong. Besides...Ethan wasn't all that bad. He was intelligent, easy on the eyes, and kind of sexy. I could do worse, I thought, optimistically.

I cleaned up, washing my tear-stained face before climbing into the bath a short time later. There, I had time to put my situation in perspective soaking in jasmine and white tea scented water long enough for my skin to wrinkle like a prune. My father never made a secret of the fact that he had always wanted a son. As pathetic as it sounded, being my father's only daughter had finally worked to my advantage. My partnership with Ethan not only helped my father but also gave me the opportunity to take a more important role in my father's business. Through Ethan I would prove I was just as capable as a son. I can be as objective and unemotional as a man. This was business, not personal.

I got out of the tub to begin my wedding toilette. After applying an ample amount of lotion and perfume to my body I styled my hair. I wore it down in layered waves with the beautiful red comb pushed into one side. I applied a light coat of blush to my cheeks, a touch of eye shadow, and added a thin coat of cherry gloss to my lips. My satin organdie wedding dress was all elegance and satin in the softest of reds.

I wondered what Ethan's reaction would be when he saw me in the dress. But he went to the chapel early, leaving a note and a small gift box on the coffee table. I read his letter, hoping to find an apology, but it was just a note informing me that a car would be waiting outside when I was ready. I opened the small black gift box. It was a matching bracelet to the comb I wore in my hair...probably Adriana's idea. I put the bracelet on and left the penthouse.

A pearl red Maybach covered with fancy wedding decorations couriered me to the chapel. When we arrived, the driver discreetly shuffled me in through the back of the building. Apparently, the paparazzi waited out front for the next celebrity sighting or wedding party. I was hardly a celebrity, even if my father was a public figure. I smiled, slightly amused by the driver's caution.

When we entered the wedding chapel I was met with oohs and aahs by the other couples. We made it just in time for our ceremony, with only two couples before us. I was summoned from the bridal room after a half hour wait. I heard the wedding song and peeked around the corner. Ethan stood at the other end of the room with the minister designated to officiate our wedding. I took a deep breath and marched down the aisle. Ethan had his shoulder length hair trimmed and wore a tailored black suit. He was admittedly, strikingly handsome, especially with a clean shaven face.

He watched with an air of cool as I marched toward him. I carried a small bouquet of red Hypericum berries, roses, and eucalyptus flowers that had been fashioned by the wedding coordinator with Ethan's strict seal of approval. After a march that seemed to take forever, I made it to the other end of the aisle where he waited for me. The minister presiding over the wedding asked us to join hands which I did without hesitation. *How many times had Ethan held my hand today?* I was already used to the feel of his fingers encompassing mine. We faced each other and listened as the minister performed the ceremony. The man went on and on about love lasting an eternity and couples making marriage work, enduring sickness and health. The minister smiled like a doting grandfather...like he had been truly honored in uniting a young couple in "love". I felt like a fraud. When it was time Ethan and I recited our vows on cue like all the other couples who had gone before us. I held his gaze without apprehension for the first time, staring into brown eyes with flecks of hazel in them. Ethan squeezed my fingers, interlocking them with his own as the minister neared the end of the ceremony and demanded he kiss the bride. I took a deep breath, expecting an awkward peck on the lips.

Then with a feverish passion that took me by surprise, Ethan pressed his lips against mine. I surrendered to the passionate onslaught as one of his hands braced the back of my neck and the other pulled me by the waist into his arms. *Heavens, what is this man like in bed?* With my thoughts racing, I released a breathy sigh as his tongue entangled and played with mine. Ethan kissed like a man who liked to kiss and for a moment, we seemed to forget about the business arrangement and our farce of a wedding. With an irrational irritability I couldn't explain, when we parted I blamed my heated response to Ethan's kiss on the moody Romanesque chapel, the flowers adorning the pews, and the panoramic view of the city skyline. I'd simply been swept into the moment. I brushed a hand across my lips. They were still warm...

Whistles erupted in the room and the bulb from a camera flashed. I looked up, like a deer in headlights as a crowd slowly filled the room.

"You look beautiful," Ethan whispered against my neck. "I love your dress." Candlelight flickered in his eyes. He brushed the side of my hair with his fingertips.

"Who are all these people?"

Ethan sighed. "I was told by the wedding coordinator that paparazzi hang around the courthouse looking for celebrities."

"What does that have to do with us?"

Ethan glared at me like I was overlooking the obvious.

"When Donald Trump's daughter got married, the press was all over it. The same goes for the daughter of Eugene Byron."

I shook my head in near panic. "What? They can't do this. We're private citizens!"

"Not anymore. You're married to the son of a multi-billion dollar land developer. The entire business world is watching," he whispered in my ear.

Flashing bulbs from the paparazzi nearly blinded us as we pushed our way through the crowd to the waiting Maybach outside of the chapel. Then I spied him...the man in the leather jacket, wire dangling from his ear, gawking at us trance-like from the crowd. I looked away as we scrambled into the car, just as an emboldened member of the paparazzi asked where we were going for our honeymoon. Ethan told him it was a surprise and kissed the back of my fingers like a doting husband. *The man deserved an Oscar.*

I pulled the train of my dress inside and the driver closed the door. "Where are we going?" I asked, realizing Ethan was still holding my hand. I tried to pull it away but he lifted my hand to his lips, kissing the back of my fingers again. Then he dropped a bombshell.

"Your father flew all of your friends to Vegas. They're coming to our wedding reception."

"And you knew about this?" I gasped.

Once again, Ethan and my father were trying to control my life, robbing me of the opportunity to tell my own friends about the wedding. No doubt my best friend Claudia would be hurt that I had not only gotten married without telling her, but that I'd broken our pact. The two of us vowed we would never marry a rich man... especially men who reminded us of our fathers. Claudia kept her end of the deal when she married Wayne, a city bus driver a few years ago. But Ethan was a carbon copy of my father, only younger, handsomer, and foreign. These billionaire playboys were all the same no matter where they hailed from.

I bit my anger down, gazing out of the car window at the string of street lights swirling by. A strong sense of decorum prevented me from ripping his head off. I was a Byron, after all and Ethan was still a client and business partner.

"I had nothing to do with it, if that's what you're asking. You'll have to take this one up with your father."

"What did he tell them? Who did he invite?"

"He told them it was a private affair...that we wanted to do it on our own."

On our own? What decision had I made, other than saying 'I do'? Ethan and my father controlled the event from beginning to end, including our so called engagement, however short-lived that was.

"What about the honeymoon?" I fumed.

"I'm taking you to Aruba."

I tried to hide my disappointment.

"We're going to Aruba? *For how long?*"

"Three weeks. Just you and me, *Lau Po.*"

I slumped against the cool leather seats in the Maybach, completely overwhelmed. And he called me "Lau Poh". I couldn't complain this time because I was legally, Ethan's "wife".

The driver took us directly to the Marcy's, the club hosting our wedding reception. Dance music filtered through the club's open doors, its pulsating beat vibrating through my body. We were still holding hands when we walked in, our hearts aflutter, not quite sure what to expect when we saw my friends. It was the first time I'd ever seen Ethan look nervous. The club was a two story loft in a large building designed to look like a warehouse. The environment was loud with flashing red lights and a deejay, who announced us as we walked in.

"What do we do now?" I asked.

"We'll say hello to your father, and then I guess you can explain what happened to your friends."

"Dear heavens, what am I supposed to tell them?" I shrieked, in near panic.

"Explain what we agreed to tell them earlier... we've been having a secret love affair for months and decided to get married. I guess from there you'll need to make it up as you go along."

"This is so infuriating! You and my father thought of everything else, but can't figure out how to explain this to our friends and family."

Ethan shrugged. "Let them think what they want."

"It's not that easy," I sighed. "These people are important to me. We could also get in trouble, or have you forgotten about that?"

"Then let's talk to your father and see what he says."

"No. I'm not speaking to him right now." I was tired of the man. Tired of him controlling my life.

At that exact moment someone tapped me on the shoulder, but as I turned to see who it was, I was swept into an embrace. I squirmed and pushed away until I realized I was in the arms of my best friend Claudia.

"You're here!" I exclaimed, grateful to see her friendly face.

"You okay?" she asked, searching my eyes.

"Congratulations," she said, grimacing as she looked over at Ethan. "You're a very lucky man."

"Thanks." He gave her a dry look. "I'm sure the girls at the office will have plenty to gossip about at the water cooler on Monday."

"Don't be rude," I pleaded with Ethan, wondering what the exchange was all about.

"I'll go over and have a word with your father," he said, leaning in to kiss me on the cheek.

Claudia rolled her eyes as he turned away.

"Your lips are smiling but your eyes are pleading for help. Don't say a word, I already know."

Claudia hugged me again.

"I knew they were up to something!" she exclaimed, gazing at me with wild eyes. Claudia stood about 5'1" and wore her hair in a short dark pixie cut. But she was massively intimidating in her way, because she was never one to mince words.

"What are you talking about?" I asked.

"The whole thing reeks of a farce! That's what I mean. How could your father ask you to do something like this? Shame on him! I'm so pissed right now. But I had to come and see you for myself."

No longer forced to lie to my best friend, I felt like a giant weight had been lifted from my shoulders.

"Can we talk?"

"Of course, dear! Let's find a quiet corner, but make sure you say hi to everyone first. Diana is here, Patty, Gloria, Cheyenne, and your Aunt Bev. Your father invited some of Ethan's friends and a few other relatives I haven't seen before. He told me to make arrangements to fly everyone out on his private plane this morning."

Claudia worked as my father's executive secretary. Like Eugene, her father was also a wealthy businessman, but he disowned her when she agreed to marry Wayne. I convinced my father to hire her as his secretary when Claudia ran out of money and could no longer make ends meet.

Claudia and I made rounds as quickly as we could, talking to friends and relatives who all seemed genuinely happy for me and Ethan.

To them, nothing seemed amiss other than the fact that the relationship and wedding had been kept a secret. Ethan joined us for a spell and I introduced him to anyone he hadn't met before. Everyone seemed to like him… *everyone except the bride.*

Soon, Claudia and I were alone, out on the rooftop, breathing in warm Vegas air. I told her about my father's situation, and how Mr. Yu wanted Ethan to oversee the project in the U.S.

"I think I need a smoke," she said, lighting a cigarette. "You don't have to say a word. You could get in trouble for this…sometimes I don't understand your father. He gets into the dumbest scrapes. I think they're after your father's company. How else do you explain your father coercing you into marrying Ethan Yu like that?"

I shook my head, sighing. "How'd you figure it out?"

"I work for the man, honey. I knew something was up a few weeks ago when Ethan and his father came to the office. They were in and out almost every other day for weeks. Then they finally came back with a couple of high powered attorneys one day. Your Dad invited the same lawyer who worked on his divorce from your mum. I was curious, so later that day when he left the office, I peeked into a folder that he left on his desk and saw the prenuptial agreement for you and Ethan."

"And you didn't tell me about it?" I shrieked. "The only person who didn't know I was getting married was me! Claudia, this really pisses me off."

"I know hun... I didn't say anything because I figured you were in on the plan. I had no idea they would ambush you the way they did."

"You said you think they're after my father's company. That can't be right," I groaned.

"Why are my suspicions so farfetched? Why would your father insist on getting the two of you together? You told me he was in trouble, right?"

"He said we were a match and Ethan's a good guy. Besides, there's a flaw in your argument. Who would trade a multi-billion dollar business venture for me? No woman is worth that much to anybody."

"There's more..." Claudia continued, enigmatically. "This morning, Hammond Industries, transferred millions of Byron Energy stock to your father. He was about to lose his control of the company, but this put him back on top."

"That can't be right. He didn't tell me he was losing control of Byron Energy…Hammond's an American company. What does this have to do with Ethan?"

"I don't know, but it's worth looking into."

I pondered this information some more as I peered over the roof at the street below. It had to be a coincidence…

"What do you think of Ethan? Is he nice?"

"He's cute but he's exactly what you think he's like. The man is a spoiled brat! He's just like my father, but worse. He's extremely controlling and acts like it's a real marriage."

"In his mind, maybe it is."

"Don't say that," I cried. "I have more than my share of problems to deal with."

"Are you attracted to him?"

I paused, not because I needed time to think it over. I was damned no matter how I answered because Claudia knew me well enough to know when I was lying and I was in no condition mentally or emotionally to admit the truth anyway.

"It doesn't matter…" I answered, somewhat politically. "The only man I want is Danny. I can't wait until this nightmare is over."

"It will be hun, don't worry."

She gave me a hug.

"Let's get back to the party. We have a wedding to celebrate!" Claudia teased.

"Don't' remind me," I groaned, following her into the club. "Ethan's trouble, I'm not sure I'll be able to handle him. I just have to remind myself that it's business as usual. Think of it this way, it won't be the first time I took work home with me."

"I don't care how cute he is, don't give in. You know this will set womankind back a few hundred years if you do."

"Trust me, I won't. But he's sexy. Isn't he?"

"And he can't seem to get enough of you. He was practically mauling you in there."

"Hey, how about we play the drinking game? Every time Ethan grabs my hand or kisses me on the cheek, we take a shot of Patron?"

"Hell, sounds like fun to me. Let's get drunk!" Claudia said, returning to her true happy-go-lucky self. "I'm just glad you're okay."

"As long as I have my friend, I'll survive," I said, giving her a squeeze. "He's not an ogre, he just happens to be the man I'm married to, for better or worse for the next three years."

"Three years! Ay! An eternity! You poor girl. At least he's cute. If I wasn't in love with Wayne, I'd take him home myself."

"Honey, you can have him!" I teased.

Just then, Ethan sidled up to me and slid an arm around my waist. I blinked as a bulb from a camera flashed before my eyes. The photographer thanked us and moved on. Claudia looked at me and giggled. "One Patron, coming right up!" she said, buggering off to order a bottle for our table.

"What's so funny?" Ethan asked, staring after her.

"Nothing. We're gonna have a shot of Patron. Care to join us?"

"You've had enough to drink," he answered, taking the glass out of my hand. "Have you had anything to eat? I'll get something for you."

"I'm not hungry," I complained. "Have a drink with us, *please...*"

Ethan sighed. "You're drunk enough for the both of us."

"So what...you can learn a lot about a person when he's drunk," I teased.

Ethan gave me a skeptical look. "You hated my guts a few hours ago, and now you want to buy me a drink? Are you hitting on me?"

"Don't be silly! We'll be tethered to each other for the next three years so we might as well make the best of it."

"Getting drunk?"

"Having some fun!" I corrected, smiling. "We'll live like roomies." Ethan went to Yale and had the whole American college experience before returning to China, so it wouldn't be much of a stretch for him. I grabbed his hand and pulled him away to our table where Claudia had already sat the glasses next to a bottle of Patron.

"You owe me two shots," Claudia exclaimed.

"This one doesn't count," I said.

We sat at the table with Ethan draping an arm around the back of my chair. Claudia giggled and took another shot of liquor.

"This must be an American game. Am I supposed to drink when the two of you laugh?" Ethan asked. "What kind of game *is this*?"

"That's so cute," she said. "Bottoms up!"

Ethan took a shot of Patron.

"How good are you at holding your liquor?" I asked.

"I'm Chinese," Ethan said, practically beating his chest. "If I can handle *baijiu* I can survive this stuff. You're the one who will end up on your ass before the night is out."

"Good thing you have a driver."

Claudia giggled again. Ethan grabbed the bottle of Patron, poured another shot and drank it down.

"You're better at this game than I thought. But you're going down faster than the both of us. I can see it in your eyes," Claudia said.

"Not faster than this pretty woman," he replied, planting a drunken kiss on my cheek.

Claudia and I laughed again, which in turn led to the three of us taking another drink.

CHAPTER 5

The following morning brought nothing but pain and misery. Blinding sunlight flooded in through the wall to wall landscape windows of my hotel room, the warmth of its light a contradiction to the cool blast from the air conditioner. My head ached, my body was sore, and I was not only cold but naked from head to toe.

I started to get up, cringing as the pain piercing my temple, forced me back down. I felt heavy. An arm stretching across the bed hung over my shoulders like an anchor. A sickening feeling washed over me as I brought my eyes into focus and gazed at the face sleeping by my side. The last thing I remembered about the night before was stumbling into the hotel room with Ethan. I winced, unable to shake the images and memories that followed next. He reached out, as intimately as a lover, sidling so close the end of his nose touched mine.

"What happened last night?" I cringed, afraid of hearing the answer.

Ethan caressed the side of my face with his open hand, biting down on his lip in anticipation.

"You don't remember?"

Then leaned in and kissed me softly on the lips, his fingers trailing up and down my neck in gentle circular motions. I had not realized before how utterly perfect his body looked and felt, hard and masculine against my soft pillowy form. Ethan kissed the side of my neck, and suckled the skin on my collarbone as he wedged his heavy body between my thighs. I felt like a gazelle, trapped between the powerful jaws of a lion… a trap from which I'd lost all power of extricating myself. It had been too long, too many quiet nights without the physical intimacy of a boyfriend who lived on the other side of the country. Why did Ethan have to be so…*irresistible*? So strong, warm and *hard*? Push him away. Far away, quick, before it's too late!

"I don't remember anything about last night," I lied.

But my body remembered. A chill raced up my spine as I was assailed by memories of Ethan and I in bed. Suddenly, every nerve in my body was on fire. We lay, our bodies coiled together covered under a thin white sheet. The hot sticky residue on my thighs, evidence of lovemaking hung thick and hot in the air, like a pheromone that only Ethan could sense. I felt his aroused presence and wondered what kept him from acting on his primitive male instincts as my center tingled with desire.

"Because you don't want to remember," he replied, hoisting himself to his elbows. He gazed down at my face, "Why is that?"

"I was intoxicated."

"Ah-huh..."

I pushed against his chest. But the gesture was so faint, so half-hearted he barely moved. He groaned, and rubbed his aroused manhood against my opening, sending spasms of pleasure through my entire body.

"And now?"

I closed my eyes, unable to meet his passionate gaze as I fished for a reply. *How could I be so foolish?* Had Ethan known all along what I had been too ashamed to admit? I folded like a lawn chair that night because I wanted him to make love to me. An immutable inextinguishable passion had been ignited between us the moment I entered that conference room and caught him staring at my legs.

He groaned as he planted a possessive trail of kisses on my face as he wedged his hand between our bodies, coaxing his fingers inside of me. I felt a ripple of pleasure so intense I thought I was about to explode.

"Nǐ shi wǒ-de..." he whispered in my ear.

I understood the meaning perfectly.

"You are mine..." he'd stated, parting my lips just so with his tongue. In one powerful sweep my legs were around his waist, my hips slowly rising to meet him. Then he dropped a bombshell...

"If we do this, the deal is off," he said, his voice a gravelly whisper.

Eyes burning with fiery passion bore into mine.

"What do you mean?" I asked, unsure of which deal he was referring to. I didn't care anymore... I just wanted to feel him inside of me. Feel our bodies together as one. I brushed dark strands of hair from his face, and kissed his lips.

"I want a real marriage," Ethan adamantly declared.

Was he serious? Or was there some other motive in mind? Sex was one thing but why would Ethan want to be married to me? He was just as much a victim of our fathers' plotting as I was...*or was he?*

"Did we have sex last night?"

Ethan shrugged. "Kind of..."

He hoisted himself onto his elbows and stared down at my face again. My eyes pleaded to finish what we'd started. I continued to stroke him to keep him hard.

"There's no such thing, Ethan. We either had sex or we didn't."

"You want to know the story?"

"Would I ask if I didn't?"

"You really don't remember?"

He looked surprised.

"Only bits and pieces," I admitted.

Ethan kissed the side of my neck and lips.

"We were drunk when we came back to the hotel. You wanted me to help you out of your wedding dress and I complied."

"Then what?"

"You took your underwear off."

"I did not!" I cried, hot with anger.

He shook his head in disagreement.

"You did. Then you followed me to the living room. I was lying on the couch when you came in and tried to have your way with me," he faked a look like he was hurt. *"I feel so used..."* he continued, a devious look on his face.

I laughed in disbelief. "Will you please be serious?"

Ethan shook his head again.

"I'm telling the truth. You kissed me. I carried you back to the bedroom. There was some very delicious foreplay involved, we proceeded to make love but you blacked out."

"*Proceeded* to make love, but didn't have sex?"

"I believe that's what I said, ma'am."

"You sure?" I gave him a hesitant look.

"Do I look like a drunken frat boy to you? You passed out so I backed off and went to sleep. We were sloppy off our ass drunk and completely stupid last night. You don't really think I would take advantage of you?"

I rubbed my opened palm against Ethan's chest in a soothing motion until the irritated expression on his face disappeared. He gazed down at me with delicious brown eyes. I wanted to kiss him all over.

"I think that qualifies as sex even if we stopped due to my blacking out," I groaned.

"I don't consider what happened last night making love to you and I'm ready to prove it."

He kissed me again, moist warm tongue entangling mine.

"So…"

I trailed my index finger down his chest.

"Are we going to make love *now*?" I whispered against his lips, a bit more eager than I wanted to sound.

Ethan's laughed… "Not until you give me an answer…can we have a real marriage? Will you be my wife? For real, this time. No games. No business. A real shot. Just you and me, kiddo?"

I took a deep breath.

"When I'm married for real, I want to be in love, Ethan. And I want a man who is deeply, passionately, in love with me."

"What makes you think I'm not already in love with you?"

Ethan looked and sounded genuine.

I sighed. I couldn't believe what he was asking me. This was a business arrangement and a one-time roll in the hay, nothing more. The look in his eyes was so sincere I just wanted to bury my face into his chest and hide. I kissed Ethan again, hoping to make him forget. If I were to have a one night stand, who better to have it with than the man I was married to? But Ethan wanted more than that, which was like a bucket of cold water on my libido. Sex was one thing, a *real* marriage was another. A relationship built on a lie was doomed to fall apart anyway. Whatever Ethan believed when it came to our relationship didn't matter. We were not in love, we were in lust!

Sex would not only compromise the thirty-year friendship between our fathers but would also strain an already tenuous business relationship. So much had happened in the past twenty-four hours I felt like my head was spinning. He stared unblinkingly at my face like a injured puppy.

"I mean it. I can't be in a real marriage with you."

I pushed him aside and rolled out of bed, sheet wrapped around my body. He gazed up at me with a wounded look in his eyes, raking a hand through his hair in frustration. I tried albeit hopelessly, to look at his face and not at his sweaty unclothed physique. Following my line of view, he grabbed a pillow, covered his groin and rolled out of bed with an angry thud. I smothered a laugh. Ethan looked ridiculous hiding behind a pillow.

"We're already married and we're about to have sex. How can you say you're not my wife? Or is marriage only convenient when you want to share our bed? I'm not your whore, Elizabeth. Where I come from, dating and sex is a pathway to marriage. Some of us have values and believe in the sacredness of love and matrimony."

"I'm a progressive American woman," I shrugged. "We don't have to be married or in love to have sex."

"But you *are* married. There's nothing wrong with sex or falling in love with your own husband!"

"There is when you're married against your will!" I snapped, an air of triumph to my tone.

Ethan smirked and a wave of heat rushed through my body. *Good grief, I wanted this man so bad.* He looked into my eyes and I averted my gaze, flushing at the idea of Ethan reading my thoughts. With a strong masculine swipe, Ethan grabbed the bed sheet I wore and pulled me close, my chest colliding softly against his. The pillow he used to cover himself dropped to the floor at my feet.

"You were no more forced to marry me than you were forced into our bed last night."

He had a point. I was drunk but fully aware of what I was doing. But these were things I was not only unwilling to admit to Ethan, but unwilling to admit to myself. I regrouped, tightening the sheet over my chest, the thin white barrier that separated us. Through it, I could feel him pressing against me, his arousal obvious.

"I won't sleep with you until you agree to a committed relationship. That's not who I am," he continued.

"Understood. There's no sense in arguing or beating ourselves up about it. We made a mistake. Sue me for wanting to have some fun," I shrugged. "Moving forward, this marriage will be nothing

more than a contract, as intended from the start. I hope you understand."

Ethan looked astounded, then finally, an expression of acceptance appeared on his face. "Fine. We'll play it your way," he shrugged, nonchalant as ever.

"Good. We'll leave this embarrassing situation behind us and forget it ever happened. That being said, I'm gonna hit the shower... there's room for two, if you're interested," I winked.

"Thank you, but I think I'll pass," he answered, waving a hand dismissively.

I turned on my heels and walked toward the bathroom. Then with a parting look over my shoulder, I dropped the sheet to the floor at my feet before disappearing into the bathroom, leaving a confused and sexually frustrated Ethan to his thoughts.

Moments later, as I stood under the hot stream of water pouring out of the shower, I replayed my argument and short-lived tryst with Ethan in my head over and over again wondering why I had even gone there in the first place. Like a drunken sorority girl I'd thrown myself at him without bothering to think of the consequences. In one night, I managed to blur the carefully drawn line separating our

business relationship and fake marriage. Why? He was everything I avoided when it came to men. I'd always been attracted to tall, handsome, working class guys who didn't remind me of my extremely wealthy father. They made me feel safe...loved. Daniel didn't have an agenda, unlike Ethan. So why was I so drawn to this man? Was it the fact that he was young and hot with a cool playboy devil-may-care persona? I was used to arrogant young men with money they neither earned nor deserved. I'd grown up with far too many self-entitled brats. But Ethan was different. The way he wore his masculinity like a badge...the smoldering intensity in his eyes. I'd seen him looking at me from afar many times in the past, his gaze protective and watchful...even a bit possessive, only I had yet to identify what those looks meant. The two of us being only the children of our parents, I thought of him as a big brother, because of the bond our fathers shared. But Ethan's silent vigilance had been much more. A nagging feeling forced itself to the forefront of my thoughts. Was the business deal a necessary invention to bring the two of us together? If so, how long had our fathers conspired to make this possible?

I quickly dismissed my suspicions, and stepped out of the shower. In this day and age an arranged marriage simply wasn't possible. Especially when it came to a forward-thinking man like my father. On the other hand, this was the same guy who secretly longed for a son.

I left the bathroom wearing only a bath towel and went to the bedroom, half expecting to see Ethan there. The comforter on the bed was in disarray, the only evidence that last night had ever happened. I draped my body in a hotel issued bathrobe, walked to the living room and looked around. The suite was empty and Ethan was gone. I walked to the bedroom again and checked the closet. His clothes were still there.

A few minutes later the door opened and room service arrived with food I didn't order. After a decadent spread had been laid out on the table, room service left and I sat down to eat. I was in the middle of pouring a cup of coffee and setting a croissant on my plate when the door open and Ethan finally walked in, wearing a jump suit and a pair of sneakers, his body covered in sweat. He quickly disappeared into the bedroom. A few minutes later I heard the shower.

I grabbed the paper, which sat on the table and started reading the news. I found one of our wedding pictures in the business section with an announcement that we had been married.

"Thirty two year-old Ethan Yu of AmeriAsia and Elizabeth Byron, daughter of Byron Energy oil tycoon Eugene Byron, were joined together in marriage...blah blah blah."

I snapped the paper closed wondering if Danny had already heard the news. Should I call and at least *attempt* to explain myself? Ethan walked in just as I was setting the paper on the table next to my plate. Dressed in dark slacks and a pale blue button down shirt, he leaned across the table, reaching over my head as he grabbed the orange juice and collapsed on the seat beside me as he drained the entire glass.

"Did you see the wedding announcement in today's paper?" I asked, skimming the front page.

"Ah huh..."

His hair was still very wet and his complexion pallid from strenuous exercise. I closed my robe, where it had fallen open like there was something to hide.

"What time is our flight to Aruba?" I asked.

I reached for a slice of fruit and Ethan reached for it at the same time, the side of his hand grazing mine. I withdrew from his touch like it burned and pushed away from the table.

"I canceled our flight."

"Why?"

"Your father told me you hated the beach. You should have said something."

"I didn't think it mattered," I shrugged.

Wasn't like anything else did…or like I had any say-so in the events concerning our wedding…

"Of course it matters," Ethan replied, a surprised look on his face. He spun his chair around and leaned towards me, gripping my shoulders with firm hands.

"I know this marriage isn't what you wanted, but I'll do my best to make life as easy for you as possible. If you want something, just ask."

"I don't need anything from you. I have my own money."

He gave me a dour look. "I'm not talking about money, Elizabeth. I'm talking about happiness. I'm sorry about what happened this morning. It won't happen again."

"Oh, but I want it to," I replied, smiling mischievously. "Speaking of favors, I think we both know what *I* want," I teased.

I bit my bottom lip and gave him my best '*come hither*' look.

"Then you should be prepared to accept everything that goes along with it."

Ethan released me then leaned back in his seat again, quickly changing the subject. "We should go to Paris. Your father said you'd like that."

"Thanks," I replied somewhat sheepishly. "I *would* like that, actually. I haven't been in years. I've been far too busy with work. The budget committee will be out to look at your designs today. I know we're supposed to go on our bogus honeymoon, but there's a bit of a time crunch."

"Where?"

"I booked conference room L454. Why?"

Ethan strolled across the living room and flipped his laptop open. "You mind if I sit in?"

I studied his movements. I was *really* attracted to this man. He turned, piercing dark eyes peering quizzically into mine.

"Negative. The meeting is *only* for the budget committee," I answered, circling the sofa to meet him on the other side of the room. "I'll go over it with you after we draft a preliminary budget proposal. You have nothing to worry about... I handpicked the committee personally. Your designs are beautiful, but..."

I let my fingers slide across the back of the sofa, seductively.

"We need to think about how much it will cost to implement."

"We'll worry about that when you prove we can't do it on a thirty million dollar budget," Ethan said, cutting me off.

I gave him a hopeless look.

"I've seen your work, Ethan...it's brilliant. It's eccentric, it's grand...some of the best architecture I've ever seen...it's *art*. I was very *very* impressed. But I think our focus should be the interior. Like I said, we'll go over the budget this afternoon and get back to you with estimated costs."

"You should have invited me to the meeting," he said, pointing his finger. I need to be a part of the process."

"And you are!" I answered, sweetly. "You're designing a multi-million dollar luxury hotel."

"I'm also a major investor. Or did you forget that? I need to know where my money is going. You work for me, not the other way around."

I slid my fingernails up his arm seductively. "Correction. I *work* for my father."

Ethan caught my wrist before my hand crawled up his chest. We locked eyes, like bulls about to lock horns.

Ethan vowed to resist a physical relationship if I didn't agree to a real marriage. I wanted to see how long *that* was going to last. He parked his hands on

90

my waist and pushed me away, eyes brimming with sexual heat. But I slid my fingers under his collar, slowly unbuttoned his shirt, and kissed him on the neck. He froze, breath catching in his throat.

"We'll go over the details on our so called honeymoon. When are we leaving?" I purred.

"In two weeks," he answered, fastening each button again. I watched as he slid fit arms into his jacket, my eyes drawn to the muscular swell of his chest. He started toward the door then turned back on his heels like he was forgetting something, and kissed me. It was only a peck on the lips, but a kiss nonetheless.

Judging from the determined look in Ethan's eyes, I had a feeling he wasn't about to take no for answer on the meeting. So as soon as he left, I called my secretary and told her to cancel the meeting at the hotel and to book a conference room at the Concord Business Center. Ethan was more concerned with his designs than staying on budget. My job as head of finance was to keep costs under control. But after reading Ethan's outline, and going over his blueprint for a six story 150,000 square feet building, there was no way we could build it for an obscene amount of money. I was going to budget the new Gold Dust Hotel down to the last nail, starting with its size, which I would slash from 150,000 square feet to 135,000 to get our budget down to 20 million dollars, where it belonged.

With the blueprint unfurled and spread across the boardroom table two and half hours later, I made a box around the area we would cut from the design with a big red Sharpie. I passed the marker to Hirsch, a bald forty-four year old finance executive from our Atlantic City office. As I leaned over the table I couldn't tell if he was cross-eyed or staring down my silk Chanel blouse. I flattened the fabric with my hands, smoothing wrinkles away from the soft crisscross designed top as I strutted across the room, sat on the edge of the table, crossing my legs, listening as the team debated budget concerns over coffee and bagels.

Reports were passed to the end of the large Maplewood table where I collected them. Diane, a bright but serious young woman in her late twenties had ascended the ranks of the company quickly, her strict hard-working attitude making her a contender for upper management. Her style of dress was as austere as her personality, which made her well liked by everyone except her immediate peers. She spoke, but only when she needed to, so I was surprised when she gave me her report, and said,

"I found a company in South America that could provide lumber for half the price listed on AmeriAsia's budget proposal."

"Is that in your report?"

"On page five," Diane answered. "I made a few other suggestions as well."

"I'll be sure to review and get back to you after I go over your assessment with Ethan. AmeriAsia's cost submittal does seem a bit over-inflated," I answered.

"We could cut costs by several million if we hire non-union construction workers," Hirsch offered.

"That's a great idea. Of course, we're obligated for a number of reasons to hire union workers. But we'll hire non-union whenever we can as often as we can to cut back on costs. As it stands, the current budget is so out of control, if we don't scale back the project will go bankrupt before we break ground. I'd much prefer to spend the bulk of our funding on the hotel interior, where guests spend most of their time anyway. I have a contractor bidding at half the cost that AmeriAsia and Byron Industries is willing to pay. But again, I'll need to run this by Ethan since he's overseeing the project."

Gary, an attorney who had come from my father's office uninvited the second he heard about the meeting, leaned across the table trying not to wrinkle his Armani business suit. I hated working with my father's staff. Especially arrogant SOBs like Gary who believed I'd gotten my job at the Gold Dust through nepotism because life had apparently, been handed to me on a silver platter. No one knew how hard I worked to prove myself to my father or the fact that I would never be as valuable to him as a son.

"You sure the changes to this proposal will go over well with Eugene? He told you to oversee the budget, not butcher it. Drawing up new contracts could take weeks."

"I apologize for making your life a little harder, but Eugene told me not to let our budget get out of control and that's what I'm doing. Let me worry about what my father thinks. You're not supposed to be here anyway," I turned away, taking a deep frustrated breath before addressing the rest of the room.

"Diane, I want an itemized breakdown on the cost of supplies, including the lumber supplier in South America in two weeks. Hirsch, you'll give me an extensive report comparing union and non-union contractor fees. Look into whether or not it's feasible to work through their buyer or supplier, I'll also need to look at all of the bids that are coming in from local contractors."

This opened a floodgate of suggestions from Diane and Hirsch, with Gary glaring at his legal sized yellow notepad as he listened in, scribbling notes. Then he finally looked up, focusing his razor sharp grey eyes on the other side of the room. I had been so engrossed in the meeting I didn't hear Ethan when he walked in. Gary stood, shaking Ethan's hand as he approached the table looking over the sprawled out blueprint, a storm raging in his eyes. I gripped Ethan's elbow and pulled him aside.

"What are you doing here?" I asked in a hushed voice. "I told you the meeting was for the budget committee."

Ethan's jaw tensed as he shirked out of my grasp. "I'm overseeing this project therefore I have a right to be here."

"Not today!" I snapped. "This is my meeting, and my staff. Let me do my job."

"And how about you let me do mine, which is managing you! I'm in charge of this blueprint, in case you forgot, I'm the one who designed it…"

"All you seem to care about is showing off your fancy structures. We don't have the funds for a

150,000 square feet building, unless you plan on pulling the money out of your butt!"

"You're in charge of finance. If we don't have the money, find some and get it done."

Ethan swiped the blueprint off of the table and rolled it back into a scroll, tying it with a band when he was done.

"We're not in China. You don't snap your fingers and expect things to fall into place. We don't construct buildings with structural problems or roads that collapse under their own weight either. We need a solid budget for the best materials money can buy. Help me *help* you."

I'd seen pictures of fallen apartment complexes, roads, and sidewalks in China on the internet. Ethan had been educated at some of the finest schools, and I had no doubt of the quality of his work. But the process moved slower in the States while buildings in China were knocked down and built anew overnight.

"Exactly how much experience do you have building hotels? Much less, designing one?"

"You read my corporate profile," I snapped, lips clamping together tightly.

Ethan loosened his tie as he around the table to my side of the room.

"I think I know more about you than what's in your public profile, Elizabeth," he sneered, correcting my all-too-obvious slip. "Which is precisely, why I feel some oversight is needed... there are also codes and licensing to consider, which you know nothing about."

"I did my research. I know what I'm doing," I shot back. "My father wouldn't have hired me for the job if I didn't."

"If you say so," Ethan retorted, seating himself at the head of the boardroom table.

I looked around the room at the faces staring back at us. Hirsch tapped his pencil on the table, glancing down at his notes as if wishing he were anywhere but the conference room while Gary looked toward the window, trying to mask the smirk plastered across his impish face.

"Your father and I reviewed the bids and have already decided on the contractors and suppliers we prefer to use," said Ethan, tersely. "I want an itemized rundown of the budget next week, *Elizabeth*. If we're over budget, I'll make a decision at that time as to whether changes are warranted or if there is additional money needed for the project. Until then, I expect an invitation to all project related meetings, any changes to the budget requiring my explicit written approval."

Even Diane looked mortified, her face turning a deep shade of red. Who would dare speak to Eugene Byron's daughter like that? She turned her eyes away, looking down at her lap, as if praying the whole embarrassing debacle was over. Newlyweds weren't supposed to act like this. Was it an affront to a man like Ethan for a woman to hold her ground in the boardroom? I suppose I was also a bitch for telling him the truth.

As I sat for dinner with Hirsch later that night over burgers and a second round of beer, absently tracing my fingers across the red and white checkered table cloth, I wondered what Ethan was so angry about in the first place? I was just trying to do my job. *Why do I feel so guilty?*

"You have to understand," Hirsch was saying, "When it comes to women, powerful young men like Ethan have to be in control, especially in front of his peers. Imagine how he feels... beautiful new wife telling him his designs aren't good enough." Hirsch flicked ashes from his cigarette into a nearby ashtray.

"Don't you *dare* empathize with him," I chided. "I told him the meeting was for the budget committee and he came anyway. He put himself in that situation. Would Ethan have a problem with my suggestions if I were a man? I'm never going to be one of those pathetic trophy wives. He needs to get over it."

I had a soft heart when it came to family, but I was a pit-bull in the boardroom. My record as VP of Executive Finance at the Gold Dust Hotel was unblemished and I planned to keep it that way.

"Ethan Yu and his father have been to the office a few times. Everyone was shocked when they heard the two of you had gotten hitched."

"Then I suppose they won't be as shocked when we get a divorce. That's usually the way it works, right?"

Hirsch coughed and choked on the cigarette smoke billowing out of his mouth. He rubbed the butt into a nearby ashtray, shaking his bald head emphatically.

"Divorce? You just got married... "

"I'm being facetious," I droned, waving my hand dismissively. "Why should I apologize for doing exactly what my father would do in the same situation? That's why he put me in charge, right?" I bit down on my bottom lip, trying to hide the uncertainty in my eyes.

"Exactly," Hirsch smiled, resting his hand atop mine. "Thought you were going soft on me for a minute there…the last thing you need to do is apologize for doing your job. Stand your ground!"

"You're not just buttering me up are you?" I pouted.

Hirsch shrugged… "Well, just a little…" he leaned in conspiratorially. "I'm trying to get in good with the boss' daughter so I can get that promotion I'm after. You hear that? *Pro-mo-tion!*"

I tapped Hirsch on the arm playfully, laughing for the first time in days. Suddenly, his eyes went cold. "Uh oh…look what the cat dragged in…"

"What's wrong?" I asked, turning in my chair.

Hirsch nodded toward the bar. Ethan was headed in our direction. I drew my hand away from Hirsch as he approached, his serious drop-dead gorgeous gaze centered on my face.

"Can I talk to you?" he asked.

"Sure. Care to join us?"

Ethan wasn't having it.

"You mind?" he replied, looking over at Hirsch.

I nodded, signaling that it was okay to leave. Hirsch grabbed his plate and took it to another table, Ethan sitting in his empty chair.

"Care to explain what happened today?" I finally asked, folding my arms across my chest.

"We're supposed to be a team but I feel like you're working against me," Ethan complained.

"I'm not against you and we *are* a team. I want this project to be a success," I told him, earnestly.

What I didn't tell him was how utterly desperate I was to prove I could take care of the company. How Eugene couldn't bring himself to trust me to bear the tradition of taking over the family business and how much that hurt.

When I was little girl my parents argued about my future. My father had decided to marry me off to some family before I had even hit puberty, as if getting married was my sole purpose in life. My mother was against it. My father hated the blue-blood families who moved in and out of our social circles, 'inbreeds,' he called them, who intermarried with other bluebloods with hopes of keeping their blue blood blue and old money old. Did he think he was different because I married a wealthy foreigner?

"And what about our *other* project?" Ethan asked, snapping me back to the present.

I gave him a bewildered look. I was still preoccupied with thoughts of Eugene and my mother.

"Our marriage?" Ethan continued, mystified, like I was supposed to know what he was talking about.

"I'm not talking about *us*, I'm talking about work!" I snapped, miffed that he was changing the subject again… angry that like my father, he refused to listen to *my* ideas.

Ethan raked a hand through coal black hair.

"You know what? Forget it!"

Before I could respond, he was already out of his chair, headed toward the door. I rummaged through my purse for my credit card and waved the waitress over to my table for the bill. But the old redhead took her sweet time, and when she finally arrived, Ethan was long gone.

After leaving the restaurant I went back to the hotel where I paced the bedroom, waiting for Ethan to return. I waited until the sun went down, until flickering neon lights from flashing signs painted the walls a sinister rainbow of blues, greens, yellows and reds. I also tried his cell phone but he turned it off, so I couldn't get through. Simmering, I finally fell asleep just before midnight, but not before locking

102

the bedroom door. About two in the morning I heard the doorknob jiggle, followed by the drunken slur of Ethan's voice, begging me to let him in.

"Come out and talk," he said.

But I ignored him, pulling the sheet over my head as he rattled around the living room making noise into the early hours of the morning.

After a restless night I took an early shower then sat before my laptop dressed in only a bath towel...one of the many perks of working away from the office. I wrote a letter to Eugene and Mr. Yu with hopes of convincing them that building a 150,000 sq. ft. hotel would cost too much money. I then emailed the letters to my secretary with orders to print and ship by one day express to the two men. My inbox was at capacity, so I went through them one by one. I answered an email from Hirsch, who wanted to know if everything was okay. I wrote back, assuring him that I was fine. Diane had also emailed to tell me she found a local contractor willing to work for half the price of the larger more expensive company my father and Ethan wanted to hire. I told her to tell Gary to draw up a contract. After I review the details, we'll get it signed whether Ethan liked it or not. It had been decided. I was going to do my job.

When I was done I ordered bacon, fruit, juice, croissants, and waffles from room service, then opened the bedroom door to remove the "do not disturb" sign from our suite...but not before scanning the living room for Ethan.

He lay spread-eagled on the sofa, fast-asleep. *Nude.* I had yet to decide whether it was obnoxious or sexy. *Even angry, I leaned toward the latter.* Ethan had obviously crawled in drunk as a skunk, his clothes from the night before strewn all over the floor. I followed the trail, collecting the items one by one before dropping them into a basket that would be taken to the cleaners. There was also a half empty bottle of vodka tipped over on the countertop. I wiped the spillage from the floor, brewed a pot of coffee, then moved to cover Ethan with a blanket I found in the linen closet. I stood over the sofa, bedspread in hand, gazing down at his ridiculously handsome physique, muscular, strong and sizeable in all the right places. Suddenly, his eyes sprang open. Hot with embarrassment and startled out of my senses, I dropped the blanket to the floor as he pulled me down.

He groaned as I sunk into his embrace, settling my toweled body between his thighs as his hands moved sensuously up and down my spine. I quietly traced the lines of his strong angular jaw with my fingertips and snuggled close, relishing his warmth and the smell of his manly flesh, enjoying the quiet between us. The faint smell of liquor was still on his breath as I nuzzled my nose into his neck and closed my eyes. When Danny held me in his arms it felt rehearsed, like a staged romance. With Ethan it was different. *Familiar.* The only thing that felt staged about our relationship was our marriage. Everything else felt right. Why didn't I see it before?

Warm lips pressed against my forehead as I settled in… thinking about my inexplicable attraction to this man and the dangerous game we were playing. His hands slipped under my bath towel and squeezed my backside firmly as I straddled him. I had Ethan right where I wanted him, inching close, my thigh chaining his leg to the bed.

"Get off," he demanded, trying to sound firm as he pushed me away.

"Why?"

"We can't do this," Ethan continued, clearly struggling to resist.

He let my legs drop to the sofa cushion as he moved aside. I sat up.

"You can't keep doing this to me!" I snapped.

Ethan lowered his head. "You're attracted to me, I'm attracted to you… I get it. But I want more."

What he wanted was a real marriage... *Stubborn bastard*. Ever hear of casual sex? Why couldn't Ethan understand how difficult it was to accept a marriage that had been patched together in a boardroom? By our fathers, no less...

"Fine, forget it!" I griped, removing myself from the sofa.

I rolled the towel around my body, physically and emotionally spent as Ethan gathered the blanket from the floor and bunched it together on his lap. I removed the "Do not disturb" sign from the door of our hotel suite, recalling why I had gone into the living room in the first place, wishing the diversion had never taken place. I was so over him!

Room service arrived a few minutes later. I answered the door dressed in a summery floral dress, as I pulled the tray inside and ushered the server away after handing him a tip. I then laid the spread on the table then piled my plate with bacon, cheese, and croissants before disappearing into the bedroom again. A half hour later, I heard plates clinking softly, then the sound of the morning news on television, the volume slowly rising until it was just right. I closed my laptop, sat my food aside, and opened the door. Ethan looked up as I strolled to the kitchenette and poured us both a cup of coffee, delivering them to the dining table where he read the paper and watched TV. I was used to making breakfast at home growing up in the house alone with my dad. We'd have breakfast together, even if he didn't come home for dinner. I continued to prepare breakfast every morning ever since.

Ethan was shirtless, dressed in the navy blue slacks he'd worn the night before, his hair a sexy disheveled mess, dark rings encircling drowsy eyes.

He accepted the coffee, his fingers covering mine in the transition as he muttered a quiet, "Thank you," eyes focused on the news.

I took a sip of coffee and stole a glance at Ethan from over the rim of my mug. He finally sat his newspaper down then turned the television off.

"We need a mediator," he said, a thoughtful expression in his eyes.

"You mean a marriage counselor? Jeez, Ethan we've been married less than a week and we're already in trouble."

"And who do you think your father will blame for our failure? Certainly, not me."

Ethan blew the surface of his coffee before taking a sip.

"We should have the marriage annulled and call it a day," I whispered.

107

He smiled.

"The judge would never agree. We've already consummated the marriage."

"Why are you so intent on making this difficult?" I pleaded.

"Because your father's empire will collapse if we disappoint."

I met Ethan's steely gaze. It was the most serious I had seen him look.

"Is that a threat?"

He shook his head slowly. "I'm not interested in business, Elizabeth...I only want what was promised to me."

I sat my cup down.

I don't understand."

Ethan clutched the coffee cup and saucer in his hands as he leaned back in his chair, crossing his legs. His soft dark hair glistened in the light like it had been coated in a slick of black oil.

"I took *great* offense to your criticism of my skills as an architect and businessman, as well as your observations about China yesterday..." Ethan's face darkened as he spoke. "Then it occurred to me that perhaps, your father shared even less than I originally thought about our families, my past, and our futures."

"Is there something you want to tell me?" I asked Ethan sweetly, growing tired of his protracted explanation.

"Elizabeth," he whispered, leaning in. "I want to fix on our relationship and I'm willing to put in the work if you are."

Ethan's face brightened, the tone of his voice shifting considerably. He sat his coffee down and lifted a flower from a vase at the center of the table, and placed it before me.

"Care to join me for dinner tonight?"

I was held captive by his mesmerizing, enigmatic gaze.

"I got time to burn," I answered coolly. What do you have in mind?"

"Dinner...a night on the town... I dunno, I'll figure something out."

I slid my hand over his. "Should I wear something special?"

Ethan held my gaze for a moment then withdrew his hand from my grasp. "Wear whatever you want," he said, rising from the table.

If Ethan wasn't interested in doing business with me or my father, then what was he doing here and why was he so interested in the hotel and Byron Energy?

Where did I fit into his plans? I was looking forward to our date and finally getting some answers.

I ordered a navy blue Herve Leger bandage dress with cap sleeves through Adriana's web site and had it hand delivered to my hotel suite. The Herve Leger dress was probably one of the sexiest dresses I had ever seen. It left nothing to imagination as it clung to every curve of my body. I pulled my hair back, twisting it into an elegant up-do, then carefully applied my makeup until it was just right…perfect for a night on the town.

Ethan was out, as he had been for most of the day. At eight, feeling impatient I assumed it would be a late dinner, if at all, when a knock drew me away from the landscape windows and my view of the bustling nightlife below.

"You're late," I said, flinging the door open.

"*I'm sorry.* I'm here for dinner with Mrs. Elizabeth Yu. Is she available?"

I sighed, folding my arms across my chest. "I'll have to check my schedule, seems I already have a date. He was supposed to be here at seven. But I'm starting to think he's a bit of a jerk."

Ethan extended an elbow. After a pause, I finally accepted, linking my arm into his as he pulled me out the door. We went downstairs to an extravagant

110

five-star Italian restaurant near the hotel lobby. An entire section lit by candles had been made private, just for us. I was surprised by the amount of planning and effort Ethan had invested in our date. We sat down and ordered a glass of white wine by candlelight as we awaited our meals, soft romantic music playing in the background.

"This is nice," I finally said. "Thank you, it was very sweet of you."

Thick dark lashes lowered, a mass of dark shiny hair fanned across Ethan's forehead as he looked down, fingers grazing the stem of his wine glass. His mouth, full and plump, curled into a tiny smile. "Being married, I figured we should at least go on our first date. A proper start, right?"

"Makes sense to me. So how *is* married life?" I took a sip of wine and slid my fingers over his, hands surprisingly rough. Ethan's gaze swept across my face as he quietly drew his hand away, a golden shade of candlelight flickering in his eyes.

"We haven't ripped each other apart despite everything that's happened, so I guess that's a good thing."

"I'm sure you've thought about it."

The look he gave me said otherwise. The waiter arrived, placing warm slices of bread between us and chilled plates for our salad. With a wave from Ethan, he refilled our wine glasses with Chardonnay.

"So… what's his name?" Ethan asked, eyes turning mysteriously dark.

"Come again?"

"Your boyfriend?"

"My *ex*-boyfriend," I corrected.

He took a breath as if bracing himself for information he didn't want to hear.

"What happened?"

"You."

"He read the paper?" Ethan asked.

"I'm breaking up with him."

"Why?"

"It's unfair to continue our relationship under the circumstances."

"You told me you love him."

"I do. Just not enough. Not the way he deserves to be loved and I don't want to hurt him. How could a woman who calls herself deeply in love with a man, marry someone else? Even under false pretenses?"

Ethan shrugged. "I don't know."

"Exactly. Real love is something you fight for, not something you give up for money. If I was truly in love with Danny, I never would have married you."

"So why did you?"

"To help my father."

"Your father is a powerful man."

"Ergo, he doesn't need my help?"

The waiter arrived with dinner and set our plates before us. Ethan stuck his fork into a pile of spaghetti covered in parmesan and sauce, twirling it around before he finally took a bite.

"Was marrying for business reasons a 'progressive American woman' thing?"

I picked at my lasagna before finally lifting my eyes to meet his brooding gaze.

"We'll call it a progressive *Elizabeth*, thing."

"Progressive until you're standing in front of your father, always at his beck and call, his go to man… what are exactly are you trying to prove?"

I shoveled two more scoops of lasagna into my mouth.

"You don't understand."

Ethan's eyes burrowed into mine…"I understand completely. I have a father too."

"But he didn't ask you to marry someone against your will. *Or did he?*"

"I make my own choices and so do you," Ethan answered.

"Fair enough." I threw my fork down. "I'm full."

"Care to walk it off?"

"Business as Usual"

I couldn't eat thinking about everything we talked about so Ethan summoned the check. We went for a stroll along the Strip, where hot neon flashing lights blinked manically around us and large architectural wonders dominated the sky. Ethan shoved his hands into his pockets, not daring to hold mine as he had done before. He stared ahead, oblivious of the chaos and nightlife surrounding us.

"A nickel for your thoughts," I said, nudging him with my elbow.

"How about a cool billion?"

"My pockets aren't deep enough. Not sure if my father's are either. Times have changed."

"Not as much as you think."

He tugged my arm, pulling me close.

"No man will ever mean as much to you as your father, will he?"

We stopped mid-sidewalk, facing each other. I stood on my toes and leaned as close as I could to Ethan's face. "It's hard to explain."

"Try me."

He cupped my chin, dangerously hypnotic eyes gazing down at my mouth, our faces tilting, ever closely. Then we started walking again, bodies shoulder to shoulder.

"When I was twelve years old my mother ran away with her lover and I never saw her again. My father is the only family I have." I tried to hide the hurt in my eyes, but I could tell by the sympathetic expression on Ethan's face, that he'd seen straight through me.

"I'm sorry to hear that," Ethan said, linking his elbow through mine. I tried to shrug him off but he held firm.

"My father gave her millions in the divorce settlement on the condition that she stay away from me for the rest of her life. So she signed away her parental rights and never came back. I hated him for it. Until I realized, he did it to expose her. To show me where her priorities are."

"So the only person in the world who ever loved you was Daddy, and now you feel obligated to pay him back."

"Something like that. I won't disappoint him like she did."

"Afraid of disappointing him or afraid *of* him?" He lifted a brow.

"Why would I be afraid of my own father?" I snapped. "You're the one who's scared! Just like everybody else."

"I'm more afraid of his daughter."

Ethan came to a stop in front of me. I parked my hands on my hips, lifting my chin defiantly. "You should be. I always get what I want."

Ethan brushed an errant strand of hair away from my face, fingers pausing to softly caress my cheek, tracing down the side of my neck.

"Spoken like a true Byron. You'll get what you desire *eventually,* Elizabeth…just not on your terms."

"Is that what happened between you and Daddy? He got a contract and you won a green card and a little *guanxi?* "

"Not at all. I'm not interested in moving to America. At least long term…"

Now we were getting somewhere.

"Then *what* was the point getting married?"

"You."

"Me?"

Ethan sighed. "One day we're going to have a talk."

"About what? *The birds and the bees?*"

"I thought I gave you a lesson in that last night?"

"Touché."

Ethan's fixed his gaze on the sidewalk. He was quiet, but there was an amused look in his eyes.

"I'm going back to China someday. But it's nice to get away. I'm not exactly what you'd call welcome, in my country."

Ethan tucked his hands into his pockets and his jaw tensed. For a moment I thought I saw tears welling up in his eyes.

"Decades ago, before you and I were even born, my father was one of the first rich businessmen in China. He started as developer of course, building high rises and apartment buildings for years, before winning a major government contract to build an apartment complex in Shanghai. One day, four years later, one of the buildings collapsed crushing hundreds of people to death. The people were rightfully very angry, many of them looking for their loved ones, many of them demanding answers from my father. He was arrested and sent to jail. In China, malfeasance that results in loss of life is punishable by death. My father couldn't explain why the building collapsed…toppling like a block of Lego's' until he hired an outside expert who determined that an inferior metal had been used in the building's infrastructure. The judge in the case dismissed the charges against my father after he produced documents that proved he had actually purchased stronger materials from a contractor who he learned had cheated him. As it turns out, the contractor had used the same inferior metal in numerous projects around the city, all of which had collapsed over the years. Needless to say, the contractor and his men were sentenced to death for their actions. But it was too late. My father's reputation had already been ruined. We lost face. The people hated him. He was effectively blacklisted until he met Eugene Byron."

"I think I understand why your father helped Eugene after the Byron Energy scandal. What I don't understand is why people in China hate you."

"I'm a second generation rich kid. Some people think the contractor who used the inferior steel was a scapegoat and that, as a second generation rich kid, I'm profiting from the pain of others. There are people in China who think they're above the law because of their wealth. I try to lead a normal life, but it's hard to escape the stereotypes when you're rich in a country with millions of poor people. When I was growing up people teased me, told me I was from a family of killers...that I was a killer. Hell, I wasn't even born when the building collapsed."

"I'm sorry you experienced that," I offered sympathetically, gripping his hand.

"I don't need pity. It only made me stronger. Besides, I had something else to look forward to. So I looked west."

After wandering along in complete silence, quietly enjoying each other's presence, we stopped by the Bellagio and sat near the fountains to watch the fifteen minute choreographed water show. The fountain shot spiraling water into the air, coordinated with colorful displays of light and classical music before an awestruck audience. We sat on the stone surround and finally, Ethan took my hand, entwining his fingers with mine.

"This is so…beautiful!" I cried, above the roar of water rocketing into the air.

"Not as beautiful as you," Ethan replied, swinging me into his arms. I was held captive by his magnetic gaze as our lips touched. The wild jets of water soaring above us seemed to exemplify how I felt in his arms, lips pressed against his lips, body crushed against his now wrinkled suit. I thought about all the naughty things I would do to him if he didn't push me away whenever I got too close. Suddenly, an out of control stream of water from the fountain rained on our heads like a tsunami. Ethan swung his jacket above us as I shrieked and ran for cover while lights from the fountain blinked off, shrouding the entire area in darkness.

"My dress!" I wailed, hair clinging to my face. Ethan wasn't far behind. He shook water from his shirt and jacket, laughing.

"You did that on purpose!" I cried.

"That water jet on the end was going crazy the entire time."

"My heels! My dress, my hair!" I whined.

"Take your shoes off."

"They're ruined!"

I kicked my heels off, stamping my feet down on top of cold wet cement. Ethan turned his back and squatted. "Get on."

"You want me to get on your back?"

"You could always walk barefoot."

"Fine…" I whined, begrudgingly climbing on.

I locked my legs at the ankles across his stomach as he carried me piggyback style all the way back to the hotel, which was only a few blocks away. I pressed against his muscular back, occasionally sliding my hands down ripped arms. He finally set me down when he reached the hotel lobby.

"That was fun."

"It's the least I could do."

A few hoity-toity onlookers gawked at us as we shook water from our clothes onto the floor, laughing. We took the elevator up to the penthouse suite, Ethan discarding his wet clothes as we entered, starting with his jacket which he hung on a chair, then his shirt, which he flung across the room. If the Herve Leger bandage dress was tight before, it was like a second layer of skin, soaking wet. I tugged at the zipper, twisting clumsily until I fell head-first behind the sofa, smashing my elbow.

"Ow! *Ethan?*"

He unbuckled his pants, stripping down to a pair of black underwear.

"Can you help me get this damned thing off? It's like a straitjacket."

Ethan was half-out of his underwear as I stumbled back to my feet. He sauntered across the room, unzipped the back of my dress, then shooed me away, trying not to look.

"In the bedroom… *now.*"

'Avoidance will get you nowhere," I warned.

He turned away as I inched out of the dress, stripping down to my underwear.

"Nothing to see here," I teased, parting with a sexy smile as I left the living room.

I closed the bedroom door and tossed the navy blue bandage dress on the bed, unsnapped my bra, and peeled my panties off. A cold blast of air from the air conditioner slapped my skin, covering me with chill bumps from head to toe. The door knob turned, and Ethan slunk in. My eyes slid down his six-pack and followed the angular curve of his waist down to his muscular thighs. He peeled his underwear off then reached out, swinging me into his arms. "You're driving me crazy, you know that?"

A stream of moonlight poured in through the window, flooding us in luminous pale light. I slipped into Ethan's embrace, silken flesh pressed against his hardened physique. Dark bedroom eyes flickered with desire. I gasped as he bent his head, moving to trace the swell of my breasts with his mouth, stroking them gently with his hands in clockwise and counterclockwise motions. Ethan groaned and gathered me close, his chest tightening as my hand roamed down his stomach, and further still to hold his thick slippery length until it moved in and out my palm.

With kinetic waves of pleasure flowing through us we finally moved from the door, gravitating away from the cold grip of air, finding warmth in each other's arms. Ethan's lips touched mine and between expert kisses, my feet were off the floor as we slid onto the bed. But I would be the one to object this time.

"No!" I said, pushing at his chest.

Ethan blinked, confusion haunting his dark brown eyes.

"What's wrong?"

"I'm saving you the trouble of stringing me along," I droned.

"Not this time," he answered, slowly guiding my hand away from his chest.

One look at his face and I knew he was serious. Ethan kissed me again, feverishly positioning my body until my legs were slung over his thighs, hips bearing down until his length was nestled into the slick moist warmth of my core. Moaning raptures, I clung to his muscular backside, guiding each deepening thrust, relaxing against him as he pushed deeper, and harder until I was full, clenching every inch of his manhood until I wanted to weep. Then I remembered something that no couple in throes of passion should ever forget. His wallet...

"I don't have anything," Ethan answered. "You're not on birth control?"

"Not exactly. It gave me acne so I stopped taking them."

"Just this once, I'll be careful," he pleaded.

After making love Ethan, planted a kiss on my forehead and rolled off, pulling me into the nook of his arms. His body spooned against my backside as I tried to still my quivering thighs.

"You okay?" he asked, kissing the curve of my shoulder.

I nodded, too emotional to speak.

"You sure? It wasn't too soon, was it? I didn't hurt you…"

"It's a lot to take in," I managed. "My life has changed so much…"

"We'll take it slow if that's what you want."

"We're way past slow, Ethan. We're in Hyper-drive."

I rolled over, squirming into his arms. He kissed my forehead.

"You're not upset?"

"I'm happy," I assured him, holding his gaze. A little *too* happy, actually…

I said nothing about our relationship or where we stood. I didn't want to scare him. He might push me out of bed or run screaming and running for the hills the second I mentioned the brevity of our marriage. Three years, nothing more. The man I was married to had just become my lover, in every sense of the word. But to accept Ethan completely meant I was allowing my father to control my life. *He* arranged the husband, the wedding, and the marriage and I wasn't about to let him get away with it. In a few years Ethan would get his green card and then it would be over. Whatever physical attraction we felt would be out of our system long before then which strangely, made me sad. Casting my worries aside, I kissed the tip of Ethan's nose and then his chest.

We made love again that night. And once more in the morning just before dawn. Afterwards, we lay in bed, basking in the glow of post-coital bliss for an interminable stretch of time, too wound up to sleep.

"What if..." I asked, entwining our hands together, "there wasn't a deal between Byron Industries and AmeriAsia?"

"We would still be together... eventually."

"How is that possible? You would be in China and I would..."

"Have a boyfriend?" Ethan chuckled, completing my sentence. "Fate has a way of bringing people together."

"You think we're fated?"

"*Destined,*" he corrected.

"You should have told me you were crazy *before* last night."

"I'm crazy about you," he quipped.

I hooked my arms around Ethan's neck and draped my leg over his hip.

"I can live with that," I purred.

He drew me into his arms and kissed me as if it was the most natural thing in the world for us to do. I looked at the digital clock on the nightstand. It was well after 7a.m. Where had the time gone? With Ethan's arms locked around my waist I stared ahead, eyes transfixed on the ceiling wondering if we were thinking the same thing. What would our fathers say about our mixing business with pleasure? They wouldn't know. They *couldn't* know. Not if I could help it.

Somewhere between eating takeout, working, and making love we finally managed to get some sleep. Then we were up again, exhausting ourselves on our laptops and cell phones eventually sleeping the hours away in ratty t-shirts or nothing at all, day and night blurring together. Contracts from Diane arrived a few days later by courier. I signed them quickly and sent the delivery man on his way without mentioning them to Ethan.

We left the following day for Paris, leaving our work on the Gold Dust for assistants and other staff down the company's chain of command. It was the first vacation I had in years...and for Ethan, his first vacation ever. So I stole his cell phone and made him promise not to mention or so much as think about work while on our "honeymoon".

"I *can't* think about anything else when I'm with you," he insisted, eyeing me like a lovesick puppy.

I tossed Ethan's phone into my bag after turning it off and then we were on our way.

Our two week trip to Paris went as expected. We eagerly took in popular landmarks like the Eiffel Tower and the Notre Dame Cathedral. We even walked down *Le Avenue des Champs-Elysées* and visited the *Tuileries*. Paris was as chic and elegant as I remembered, especially the gorgeous architecture, much of which had been designed from the cool cream-colored limestone that had been imported from *Oise* to destinations like the *Place de la Concord*. Overall, Paris had provided us both a much needed break.

Back in the real world, life was sailing along. Diane kept me updated on the project. I wasn't supposed to check emails or text messages, but did when Ethan wasn't looking. It was nice to come up for air every now and then. Claudia called in tears about Wayne, they were having problems. She was hysterical so I could only make out part of the story through the crackle coming my through my phone so I promised her I would visit when I was stateside again.

Two weeks later as I packed our luggage for the trip home, I flipped through the dozens of pictures I'd put in a scrapbook, wondering if the photos were memories of our honeymoon or something to have on record to prove the legitimacy of our marriage to immigration.

I stopped at a picture I had taken of Ethan at the Louvre. The man was unnaturally handsome. It was like the gods descended from the heavens to personally bless him not only with the gift of beauty, but the presence of power. In Paris, I couldn't help but notice how women stared at him, or cut their eyes sideways, a smile curling the corners of their mouths, some of them blushing, fluttering eyelashes lowering as they looked down or away, awkwardly chewing their lips as they waited for Ethan to notice them. He seemed oblivious of the attention, even from other men, who stole an occasional glance when they thought no one was looking. At our hotel, some had even ventured to ask his business in Paris, their greedy little eyes beaming with interest. A wealthy Chinese businessman…one they assumed would blindly invest in whatever scheme they'd concocted. I saw women in the background of all of our pictures, gazing over at him, *at us*. That's when I noticed the face lurking among the crowds at the *Louvre*. There was nothing unusual about this face, only that I'd seen it before. My heart raced as I flipped through the rest of album, where the same man appeared again and again, lurking in the background in several of Ethan's pictures. Someone was following us! I gasped so loudly, Ethan rushed into the room like there was a fire.

"What's wrong?" he asked, kneeling beside me.

"There's a man lurking behind you in all of your pictures," I panted, flipping through the scrapbook as I pointed out the leather-clad thug in each one.

"I saw him in Vegas at the Palazzo and standing outside at the chapel after our wedding."

"Are you sure?" Ethan asked, in an eerily calm voice.

"Of course, I'm sure. He's in several of our pictures at different locations on different days. He's obviously watching us."

Ethan shut his eyes and sighed like he was pissed.

"It's the paparazzi again," he said.

I watched as he paced around in a circle then kicked a nearby chair. He acted more like a man who was guilty of something, than someone annoyed by the press.

"Just because a handful of people on Wall Street know who we are, doesn't mean we're famous."
Ethan walked away, returning a few seconds later with a French gossip magazine. He opened it and flipped through the thick glossy pages until he found the right one. I looked at the article. There were several fashionable women, actress and models alike, and then a picture of me and Ethan with a caption written in French.

"What does it say?" I asked.

"They refer to you as the stylish daughter of business tycoon Eugene Byron."

Ethan spoke a moderate amount of French, which had been useful in helping us get around in Paris. Ethan smacked the magazine down on top of the coffee table. Seeing my picture in a gossip magazine with a gaggle of airheaded socialites depressed me.

"You okay?"

"I'm fine," I sighed, collapsing into his arms.

"What on earth were you thinking?" he asked, cupping my chin.

I blinked tears from my eyes.

"We were in danger. You said you wanted to get away from China so I just assumed..."

"Someone had been dispatched from China to kill me?"

I nodded, wiping a tear from my eye. Ethan laughed, drawing me into his arms.

"But the man in the pictures isn't a Chinese. You watch too many spy movies," he laughed.

"I was scared," I sobbed.

"Care to explain why?" he asked, echoing my words.

I shook my head. I was having a hard enough time explaining it to myself.

CHAPTER 6

I was elated when the chauffer-driven Maybach parked in the driveway of the three story beach house I called home. I rolled the window down and gazed out as Ethan leaned across my lap, lowering his shades.

"We're here," I said, answering the unspoken question in his eyes. The driver had already unloaded our luggage and was on his way around to my door when I jumped out and ran down the walkway, hauling two of the suitcases he left near the car.

Ethan climbed out of the vehicle coolly, sunglasses still covering his eyes as he surveyed the flawless landscape.

The house sat on top of a cliff overlooking the ocean in an area called Sharkfin Bay. I could hear waves crashing ashore against the craggy rocks fortifying the base of the house on the other side, spraying a fine mist of cool ocean water into the air. The driver continued to dump our luggage on the pavement one by one as I unlocked the door to the house and bumbled inside. Ethan grabbed his bags and followed, peering inquisitively around the corner of the chateau where a trail lined with boulders and wild peonies forged a cobbled path to a private beach. The backyard featured an elaborate landscape adorned with flowers, organic fruit, a vegetable garden, and a handmade gazebo as its centerpiece, my private sanctuary.

Ethan closed the door behind us as he walked inside. The blinds to the patio door had been left open by the cat-sitter, and a fresh bowl of water for Roger had been placed nearby. Hearing the commotion of my entrance he strutted in, happy to see me, meowing and circling my legs. Shimmering light reflecting from ocean waves filtered into the living room, filling it with an abundance of bright natural light. I dropped my suitcases and sighed as I gazed out the window at the stunning view. "Hello, Roger! Mommy missed you!" I said, bending to brush his soft black fur with my hands. Already bored with the attention, he lifted his tail, rubbed his chin against my leg, and walked away. I followed Roger over to the window, lifting the cute little tuxedo cat into my arms.

"I bet you're hungry," I purred into his ear, brushing his furry white neck with my fingertips.

Ethan swept a hand through his hair, watching as I sauntered off into the kitchen to prepare a plate of wet cat food for Roger. When I was done I sat the saucer on the floor to answer the ringing phone.

"I saw pictures of you and Ethan online. Very convincing," Daddy praised, after a brief hello. "I'm glad the two of you are getting along."

"Well, it's not like we had a choice," I said, cutting him off.

"I heard you were fighting."

"About what?" I droned, irritated by the judgmental tone in his voice.

"Work. I got your letter. Edgar Yu and I agree with your proposal. 135,000 square feet is sufficient."

I cut a look at Ethan from the side of my eye and lowered my voice. He was still hauling the rest of our luggage into the house.

"I'll let him know," I muttered, unsure of exactly *how* I was going to tell him. "He won't be happy about it."

"Then make him happy," my father snapped. "Don't mess this up, Elizabeth. I mean it. This is business, not personal. It'll be over soon enough."

"I know," I answered, gripping the phone. "What I don't understand is why you're acting like this. Why Ethan and his father are so important to you?"

"They're not important to me, they're important to *us*."

My heart dropped like a stone. What was he talking about?

"Is this about Byron Energy?" It was hard to keep the frustration out of my voice. Maybe Claudia was on to something about the millions in stock that came in after Ethan and I had gotten married. None if it was making any sense.

"The relationship I have with the Yu family is complicated," Dad answered, reticent as ever.

"Complicated or twisted? Just how in the hell did I get involved in your shenanigans?"

"Maybe you should ask your husband."

"He's not my husb—I gotta go," I said, as Ethan entered the kitchen.

I hung up.

"Was that your father?"

"Yes," I muttered, trying to hide my irritation.

"We have six weeks of vacation left," Ethan noted, clearly irritated that my father had called.

"So."

"What did he want?"

"He asked about our honeymoon and something or other about Paris," I hummed, crossing my legs at the ankles.

Ethan studied my face, his head turning sideways.

"Did you tell him about us?"

"No! Why would I do that?"

I knew I sounded just a tad defensive.

"I would prefer to keep our relationship private."

"They already know we're married," he smiled, following me out of the kitchen.

"I'm serious, Ethan… It's none of his damned business."

"Fine, I won't say anything," he smirked, throwing his hands up in mock defeat.

"So when do I get the grand tour?" Ethan asked, deftly changing the subject.

I eyeballed his face. He was laughing, shoulders bouncing up and down as he tried to hold it in.

"What are you looking at?" he grinned.

"Nothing," I shrugged, smiling.

"Do I look like the Mona Lisa to you? You're staring. Stop doing that. It's rude."

I covered my mouth. Now I was the one who was laughing.

"Seriously," he pressed, observing me with a perplexed expression on his face.

"What's so funny?"

"Your eyes crinkle when you laugh."

Ethan's mouth dropped in mock surprise.

"What was that? I look like an old man?" he barked.

E. Hughes

I heard the warning in his tone and backed away as I tried to keep my laughter in check. I ran up the stairs, bursting with giggles, but Ethan lunged after me, catching me halfway up the steps where he hauled me over his shoulder like a sack of potatoes.

"Where are you taking me?" I demanded, woozy from the sudden movement.

He kicked a door open at the top of the stairs.

"Where else?" Ethan answered. Then after a pause asked, "Where in the hell are we?"

"The guest bedroom!" I squealed, laughing as he dropped me on top of the bed.

"Oh. We can't do it in here," he said, rethinking his original plan.

"For the next three years we can do whatever we want!" I teased, squirming into his grasp.

"Just three years? I need an hourglass so I can count the days before you slip through my fingers."

"I'm just the girl you married for a green card," I shrugged. "What's wrong with you, Ethan? Most guys would kill for no-strings-attached sex with an attractive woman. Just enjoy it," I smiled.

"No, you're the girl I married. The girl I'm in love with," he corrected. "I think too highly of you and our relationship to reduce what we have to sex."

I swallowed nervously.

"Okay, fair enough. Although, there's just one thing I disagree with."

"Every word I said was the truth. You're not allowed to disagree," he said, smiling gently.

"You married me for a green card and we've only been married for four weeks. How can you say you're in love with me?"

Ethan took my hand in his and kissed the back of my fingers.

"Because I have been in love with you my whole life. From the moment I laid my eyes on you, even before that…"

"You know nothing about me," I said, trying to quell the nervous rumble of my stomach.

"I know you're career-driven, passionate about family, and breathtakingly beautiful. I want to spend the rest of my life with you…"

I shook my head.

"I don't know what to say," I answered, still unconvinced.

"I'll prove it. Elizabeth, there's something I need to tell you," he said, gripping my hand.

My stomach fluttered nervously as I waited to hear what he had to say.

Suddenly, a string of noisy chimes rang out. Ethan cursed the intrusion and rolled out of bed.

E. Hughes

"I'll get it," I insisted, resisting his attempts to draw me back as I skipped out of the room.

I ran downstairs, thinking it was the chauffer at the door with something we left behind. But when I opened the door, it was Danny who stood on the other side.

CHAPTER 7

"Surprise! Danny exclaimed, as I stood gawking at him, unable to speak.

He rushed inside, lifting me off the ground as he spun me around. Too stunned for words, it had taken almost a full minute before I said something.

"What are you doing here?" I cried. "I wasn't expecting you."

Danny smiled like a cat with a bird in its mouth.

"I flew in a few days ago."

My eyes were wide as saucers.

"But I was out of town. How'd you know I was back?"

"I paid your neighbor's son to give me a call when you arrived. Damn, did that pay off. You look good. I miss you," he added, looking me up and down.

"Danny, this isn't a good time. We need to talk."

"About what?" he answered. "I thought you'd be happy to see me."

"I, I am..." I stammered, suddenly realizing, Danny was no longer looking at me.

Ethan stood behind me in the foyer, legs crossed, hands in his pocket as he gazed at the golden-haired stranger.

"Hi, I'm Danny," he said, voice deepening, eyes wide with suspense.

Danny extended a hand, but Ethan ignored it, letting it drop. I felt my alliance shift. I wasn't Danny's girl anymore. I was *really* married, and Ethan was the man I wanted to be with.

"I'm Ethan Yu, Elizabeth's husband," he answered firmly.

I didn't expect him to announce it this way. I wanted Danny to hear it from me.

"I'm sorry… I wanted to tell you," I explained.

"Married?" Danny gasped. "How can you be married? Why?"

I looked helplessly at Ethan.

"Do you mind?" I asked.

"Actually, I do," Ethan answered.

"We'll talk outside," I amended. "Danny, just give me a minute to explain, okay?"

Danny backed out of the house and grabbed his suitcases, which sat on the doorstep. I closed the door behind me, leaving Ethan in the foyer with an irritated expression on his face.

Danny walked briskly to the rental car parked in the driveway, tossed his luggage in the backseat, and walked around to the driver's side.

"It's not what you think," I pleaded, as Danny climbed into the car.

"Not what I think! I just traveled across the country to find out my girlfriend married some other guy! I can smell him all over you, for chrissakes!" he sneered. Don't ever talk to me again. Got it?"

He put the key in the ignition and started the car, but I grabbed the door and pulled it open.

"Danny, it's a marriage of convenience. It's not real."

He looked up, eyes wide with disbelief.

"What?"

"It's a marriage of convenience. I tried to tell you before but I couldn't.

Danny grabbed his cell phone, dropped it into the inside of his jacket, then climbed out.

"Explain that again?" he said.

"I married Ethan to help him get a green card. He's the investor from China I told you about. Our fathers have been friends for over thirty years. Daddy asked me to help him out."

"You married a stranger for a green card?"

142

I nodded guiltily. "Only, he's not exactly a stranger. I've known him since I was a little. I wasn't trying to hurt you, Danny."

"How long do you have to stay married to him?"

"Three years, before he can apply for permanent residency. Then we go our separate ways," I answered.

"I have to wait three years to be with you again?"

"No doubt you won't be waiting alone. I understand if you want to move on."

"I'll need some time to think it over."

"Don't bother," I replied. "It's best we end things now. Like I said before, I don't expect you to wait for me. I'm sorry."

Danny nodded, then solemnly climbed back into his car.

I strode back to the house, eyes brimming with tears as I walked inside. Then I leaned against the door and quietly sobbed. I didn't expect it to be so hard.

As I pulled myself together, wiping tears from my eyes, I looked up to find Ethan in the foyer standing before me.

"You okay?" he asked.

I nodded. "I told him it was over," I said.

What I neglected to tell Ethan was what I told Danny about our marriage. But I'd only said those things to soften the blow of breaking up with him…

"I'm sorry you were forced to meet him like this. I procrastinated over telling Danny the truth because it made me so uncomfortable," I confessed.

"Breaking up with a boyfriend is hard. I understand," he answered coolly.

"We were in the middle of something before he got here. We can pick up where we left off. You were about to tell me something," I suggested, optimistically.

"Oh. *That.* Don't worry about it. I forgot what I was going to say."

I tried to decipher the frosty expression on Ethan's face, but to no avail.

And with that, he strode away, as I stood alone in the foyer wiping tears from my eyes.

That night, Ethan slept in the guestroom, and I slept in my own bed. I'd gotten used to his warm body, the feel of his arms wrapped protectively around me, and making love every day for the past four weeks, just before dawn. Did he hate me now? Did he think I was an evil bitch for sleeping with him before officially breaking up with Danny? Was he not in love with me? Moreover, was I falling in love with him?

The next morning I awoke to find a small pink gift-wrapped box on the nightstand. Inside were four pieces of Peanut butter and raspberry imported chocolate. I took one out, popped it into my mouth, then ate another when I was done. That's when I noticed the ring hidden in the box in an empty crate. I slipped the gorgeous diamond ring on my finger then modeled it, before closing the box again. Ethan strolled in a few minutes later, dressed in a bath towel. He sat on the edge of the bed and shortly after, our morning ritual resumed.

"Thank you, for the ring," I said. "And the chocolate…"

"You like it?"

"It was delicious."

"I was talking about the ring."

"It's beautiful. But I really like the one I already have."

"I gave it to you for a reason. My mother would like to see us get married in China."

"In China? Does she know about the green card?"

"I would prefer she didn't."

"One lie always leads to another until it snowballs out of control."

"When I said I loved you I was telling the truth."

"Ethan—."

He silenced me with a finger over my lips.

"We made love every day for the past four weeks."

"I know," I smiled, sliding under his arm. "What about it?"

"You don't find it strange?"

"Not really," I answered, wondering what he was getting at.

Ethan shrugged. "Never mind, then."

That night he left the guestroom and moved into my room. I guess all was forgiven. We carried on much the same way, with only a few weeks of our eight week leave from work to spare. At night, Ethan cooked dinner, and in the morning I made breakfast. I was standing over the stove, scrambling eggs one day when my cell phone rang. I recognized the number immediately then pressed the ignore button. What on earth could Danny possibly want?

He called again a few days later one morning when Ethan was out at the grocery store, picking up items for dinner. So I finally decided to take his call as I made pancakes for breakfast.

"Hello, sweetheart."

"What do you want, Danny? I really don't think we have much to say to each other now."

"On the contrary, I think we do."

"What exactly would that be?" I asked, gripping the phone.

"Come and find out."

"I can't see you anymore."

"But I have something for you."

"Not interested," I answered, cutting him off.

That's when I heard the sound of my own voice filtering through the line. It was a recording of me and Danny talking the night I told him about Ethan.

Every word of what I said about the green card had been recorded.

"As you can see, we still have plenty to discuss."

"You recorded our conversation. That's illegal."

"Marrying a foreigner for a green card is illegal. I'm just the jilted boyfriend. I'll get off easy."

"Why are you doing this?" I trembled.

"For money, of course. I thought when I married you, my days of working a regular nine to five were over."

"You were after my father's money!" I gasped.

"Is that so wrong? Is it fair that you, and people like your husband are born into wealth and I'm not?"

"We didn't choose our parents."

"Exactly. But we choose the people we're married to," he retorted. "And you chose him, thus robbing

147

me of my fortune."

"What do you want, Danny?" I asked, cutting straight to the point.

"Two hundred and fifty thousand dollars. A quarter-million will make things right," he said, in a snaky voice.

"I don't have two hundred and fifty thousand dollars just lying around."

"That's too bad," Danny said. "Immigration will have their work cut out for them. Especially when they start digging into your father's business practices to see if he violated any other ethics when he asked you to marry one of his investors. You're nothing but a whore, just like the rest of these bitches."

"You're an asshole. I really dodged a bullet when I married Ethan instead of you."

"What's it going to be, honey? Cold hard cash or five years in jail for immigration fraud? Ethan will serve time in jail before he's deported, and will never set foot in America again. Think it over."

He was right. But this was blackmail. I didn't know what to do... lives would be destroyed because I said too much to the wrong person.

"I'll work on getting the money," I muttered, dejectedly.

"Good. I'm glad we're on the same page," he answered, crisply. "I'll call you with instructions so make sure you answer all of my calls. And don't tell your husband about any of this, or *else.*"

And with that, he hung up.

I stood over the stove trembling as burning pancakes set the fire alarm off. I numbly moved the pan from the flames, fanning the smoke away. Tears streamed down my cheeks as I opened windows and the patio door.

"What's going on?" Ethan asked, as he walked in.

"I burned the pancakes."

"Oh," was all he said. "Are you okay?"

"I'm fine," I answered tersely.

"Were you crying?"

"No… it's just the smoke," I lied. Yet again.

I moved through the rest of the day like a zombie. I needed someone to talk to. Danny threatened to take the recordings to immigration if I talked to Ethan. Worse, Ethan hated Danny and acted strangely if I so much as mentioned him. There was Claudia, but she had problems of her own. I promised to see her when I was stateside again but had been too involved in my own affairs to visit.

Not long after the call from Danny, Ethan started to get his share of strange phone calls as well.

Someone calling from an anonymous phone number would hang up whenever he answered, sometimes calling in the middle of the night. I had no doubt in my mind that it was Danny, harassing us.

I received the dreaded phone call from Danny a few days later. He wanted the money in a briefcase, delivered to him in "tax free" cash, he said.

I couldn't figure out where to get two hundred and fifty thousand dollars. I had the money in my account, but it would take a week or two for my bank to process a cash withdrawal that size and Danny wanted the money in approximately three days in unmarked cash. Ethan had grown suspicious of the phone calls that often carried me into another room, as Danny taunted me with one phone call after another. He'd also noticed how reticent I was when he asked me about it.

I eventually decided to withdraw the money from the joint account Ethan had set up for both of us. His bank allowed large sums of money to be withdrawn the same day. It was a matter of getting the cash out quickly and replacing it with my own via check. The scheme made my flesh crawl. But I wanted to protect not only Ethan, but my father from Danny's plotting. I would tell Ethan when it was over and the data was safely in my hands. Though in today's highly advanced technological world, a file like that could never be destroyed. It would always exist on Danny's hard drive even if he were truly inclined to get rid of it. I wanted to go to the Feds, to tell them about the bribery and blackmail but I couldn't do it without implicating ourselves in a crime.

I went to a private office at the bank two days later with a briefcase secured by a combination lock with the bank manager who had me sign documents giving them permission to release the money.

"We'll just need your husband's signature," he said, taking the paperwork away when everything was signed.

"It's bank policy and required on all joint accounts."

I had to have the money in less than twenty-four hours. How could I get Ethan to sign the paperwork without telling him what it was for?

"Actually," I said, to the bank manager, "I'm using the money to buy a gift for my husband. It's a surprise. There's no way I can ask him to sign this without him demanding to know why. And that will ruin everything. I have to pay for the gift with cash. I have my own account, but it will take the bank two weeks to give me the money. I wrote a check to replace the two hundred and fifty thousand dollars in our joint account. Because of that, I don't think it's really necessary to have the paperwork signed by my husband."

"I see," the slick looking banker said. "Well, since you're replacing the money right away with money from your own account, we may be able to make an exception. I will call your bank to verify the availability of the funds, and that there are no immediate holds and then we'll get your cash withdrawal to you. It will be just a few minutes…"

A half hour later, two hundred and fifty thousand dollars was in my possession and the whole ordeal would soon be over. That night, about two in the morning, the phone rang as scheduled. Ethan slept soundly through the commotion as I tip toed out of the room to meet Danny at a nearby hotel. Real cloak and dagger dangerous stuff. No one knew where I was going, not even my husband. If something happened, who would suspect Danny of doing something to hurt me? But I had to finish this, for my family. The best I could do was to send an email to myself with a message:

If anything happens to me, Daniel Williams is responsible.

Then I put a code only my father would understand
"My father will know what this means…"

It was the date of my parent's wedding anniversary.

When I arrived at the rundown hotel I'd been directed to, Danny opened the door, stepping aside as I walked in. The smile on his face was a mile-wide, but the look in his eyes was pure evil.

"You got my money?" he said, as I strolled in, dressed in a long sleeved black dress.

"I have your money. Do you have the data?"

"Not so fast, beautiful," he interrupted.

I gave him the briefcase. Danny tried to pop it open, but the combination code prevented him from getting inside.

"Open it," he demanded.

"Not until you give me the data."

He tossed a thumb drive in my hands then grabbed the suitcase. I slipped Danny a sheet of paper with the codes, then watched him open it to verify that all the funds were there. Danny grinned.

"You do realize, I could have copies."

"I know that. But…you already have what you want. I would hope you won't bother us anymore."

"You're right. I don't want money from you. I want something else."

His eyes crawled up my legs, stopping when they landed on my breasts. He licked his lips and smiled, rubbing his hands together deviously.

"I'm in love with my husband," I whimpered.

"I know you are. Otherwise, you wouldn't be here. I know how much you love your family...that you would do anything for them. That's why it's so easy to manipulate you. That kind of love can only make a person weak. Now take your clothes off."

"Go to hell!" I growled, moving toward the door.

But Danny grabbed my arm.

"Fine. Then I'll go to immigration. Enjoy your freedom while you still have it," he said, as I continued to walk out. "I'll be sure to send your recording to the press. The gossips will get a kick out of it. Your father's stock will drop when the feds starts looking into his business affairs and your wonderful husband will be deported. You're going to let something like sex, ruin your family?"

I stopped short of opening the door.

Danny took his shirt off, stepped out of his pants and underwear, then tossed them on the floor. He then walked across the room, took me by the hand and led me to the bed where he lifted my dress over my head and tossed it aside

"Take them off," he ordered, gesturing toward my underclothes.

I got undressed as he moved across the room again, pulling a video camera in plain sight. I felt ill.

"On the bed, gorgeous..."

154

A tear streamed down my cheek as I weakly complied, sitting on my knees as Danny stood before me, his groin pointed at my face. Looking at him made me sick as he circled the bed, snapping naked pictures of the both of us. Compromising pictures that made it appear as though we'd been intimate.

"Smile for the camera!" he teased.

I covered my face with my hands, hiding from the glare of its lens.

"I can't do this," I cried, moving away, feeling my skin was about to slide off of my bones.

I flinched as Danny inched toward me, laughing as he grabbed my hand and slipped the new diamond ring Ethan had given me from my finger. I was being robbed. The ring was worth more than the money in the briefcase I'd given him.

"Don't worry, I'm not going to rape you," he sneered. "I just needed a bit of insurance. You and your husband better not think of coming after me. Got it?"

"What are you going to do with the pictures?" I wept, realizing how much trouble I'd gotten myself into.

"They're for my personal collection. Something to remember us by..."

155

I limped out of bed and grabbed my clothes as he put the camera away. I ran out of the hotel suite as fast as I could, carrying my shoes as I rushed into the elevator, tears streaming down my face. I raced across the hotel lobby sobbing, grateful for the late hour, and that no one had seen me.

I felt dirty. So I took a shower as soon as I got home, and slept in the guestroom. Ethan climbed into bed with me, just before dawn, a question in his eyes. I wanted to tell him what happened, I really did, but I couldn't. And when he kissed me, I turned him away, ending our early morning ritual.

I was depressed for days, as I moped around the house feeling ill, wondering if Daniel would reappear and try to destroy our lives again. I was tired of jumping out of my skin whenever the phone rang. But he never called. Then I remembered something. If I could put an ocean between us, I could make Danny go away. I broached the topic apprehensively, as Ethan sat on the sofa reading the paper.

"We have a week of vacation left. You mentioned going to China. I'm still interested if you are," I said, unable to look him in the eyes.

"You still want to go?"

"Of course!" I answered, trying my best not to sound desperate.

"Book the flight. We'll get out of here tomorrow. My mother will be happy to see us."

"I'll be happy to see her too…" I said.

I sat next to Ethan on the sofa and gave him a hug. The first time my fingers had touched him in a week.

The flight to China was over thirteen hours long and I was sick the entire plane ride. I gripped Ethan's hand as I leaned back in my seat, too nauseated to read or sleep.

"You sure it's the altitude making you sick?"

"I always get sick when I fly."

"You didn't get sick on our flight from Paris. Maybe it's something else?"

"What makes you think that?" I asked, turning in my seat to eye him directly.

Ethan shrugged. "We made love every night for more than a month and you still haven't had your period."

We made love every night for six weeks, to be exact. But we used protection… except that last week in Vegas. Nevertheless, I was embarrassed and annoyed with Ethan for paying attention.

"We have nothing to worry about. I'm irregular," I assured him.

I wasn't irregular. I was nervous. I had three pregnancy tests in my luggage and all of them were positive, indicating that I was probably pregnant. A thought I couldn't' fathom, much less even deal with just yet.

"Oh," he answered, looking a bit disappointed. "It would make my mother happy," he said.

I closed my eyes, ignoring him, my stomach churning like there was an active volcano burbling inside of it.

"Are you working?" I asked, as Ethan sifted through mail and other letters that had come to the house.

"I'm trying to get a jump start on work before we go back next week."

I sighed, trying not to projectile vomit in his face.

"Can you deal with it later?" I pleaded, certain my face was about to turn green.

Ethan nodded, stuffing the mail and the rest of his paperwork back into his briefcase before taking my hand.

The rest of the thirteen hour trip had given me time to think, especially with Ethan so being supportive as I sat beside him dry-heaving with a barf bag in my lap. I promised myself I would tell him about the blackmail, the pictures, and of course, the pregnancy tests. I grew up in a house of secrets…with parents who didn't know how to communicate and women who were taught to mind their manners. But I was tired of bottling my emotions inside. I didn't care *how* fate brought us together or the fact that we'd only been married seven weeks. I loved Ethan, and it was time to tell him. Especially now that a baby was involved. If the doctor confirmed what the pregnancy tests and my body had already told me, I was going to keep the baby. I had even spent the rest of the flight imagining what he or she would look like with our beautiful genes mixed together.

After we landed in China's Shanghai Pudong International Airport, we were met by a driver holding a sign that read Yu XiaoMing, who swiftly directed us through the bustling city airport to a black Acura outside of the terminal. China was busy, crowded, claustrophobic, and surprisingly reminiscent of American cities like New York where people were unabashedly direct. I'd only been in the city ten minutes and two people had already shoved me out of their way, calling me a fatty as they bustled through the airport with their luggage. Tensions definitely ran high. The ones who didn't point or call me a *laowai woman* to my face, stared as

Ethan gripped my hand, carefully shuffling me into the waiting car before climbing in beside me.

Was I really fat, and pregnant? *Or was I really just a fatty?* I pouted. Everyone in China was mostly skinny. I felt like a whale. No, I was definitely pregnant, I thought. It was the hormones making me feel like a walrus. We were joined in the vehicle by a man who looked like a security guard. I gazed out the car window at the towering skyscrapers and apartment buildings. It wasn't the exotic "oriental" paradise Americans saw in movies. Shanghai was truly a city that never sleeps.

Ethan hit the ground running the moment we arrived. He insisted on taking me to his apartment in a luxury development called the *Shanghai Centre*. I refused, instead following him to the factory he owned on the outskirts of the city.
"I won't be long," he promised, guiding me into the building.

When we walked in, we were greeted by an older guy with a toothless grin. He was friendly enough, as he threw fake punches at Ethan until one landed against his stomach.

E. Hughes

"Hey boss, man," he said in English. "How'd an ugly guy like you get such a pretty woman?" he smiled.

"Better be careful," another guy said. "He might sic his guards on you."

I looked around as a group of three very large, very intimidating looking men closed in on us. The first guy's name was Chan. He looked oddly familiar.

"Guards?" I asked.

"Things get crazy from time to time," Ethan explained, taking hold of a lever on one of the machines.

I choked on the fumes sputtering out of the machinery as Ethan jumped in to work with the rest of the guys. I'd noticed a permanent dark cloud over the city since we arrived. The pollution in Shanghai was as bad as the air in Los Angeles.

"These guys follow you *everywhere?*" I asked, lifting a brow.

"Everywhere I go. There's one more, but he's not here at the moment."

I swallowed nervously as the bodyguards stood around us, unsmiling. Apparently I was standing a bit too close to the boss. Chan and David were both Chinese, Michael was very tall, and very British with dark, extremely handsome complexion and the mysterious, Efrayim, was out of town.

161

After an hour of waiting for Ethan to finish checking his books, we high-tailed it out of there much to my relief, as I waved to all of Ethan's workers, who looked neither unhappy or enthusiastic as they finished the day's work.

At the apartment, I kicked my shoes off as soon as we arrived, to find my feet were drastically swollen in my high heels.

"I'm so tired I could pass out," I said, collapsing atop Ethan's square shaped sofa.

He collapsed beside me, laying his head back against the cushion.

"I would travel back and forth from the States to China more often if not for the plane ride," he complained.

"I can see why," I retorted.

Ethan unbuttoned his jacket and tossed it on a nearby chair.

"We need to talk," he said.

The expression on his face was serious.

"What's wrong?"

"Your ring for starters. I haven't seen it in over a week."

I looked down at my hands, breathing sharply.

"Is that why you've been acting so weird? Why you were distant? You lost the ring, didn't you?" he continued.

I nodded, still yet unable to tell him the truth about Danny.

"Why didn't you tell me?"

"You know my family. We're not the best communicators."

I turned my head, unable to look him in the eye.

"You can talk to me about anything. I love you, Elizabeth…"

Ethan pushed my back against the sofa and slowly unzipped my pants. His hands crawled into the lining of my panties. I moaned softly as his fingers explored the folds of my moistened flesh until it began to pulsate and throb with need.

I inched out of my jeans and dropped them to the floor as I waited anxiously for Ethan to finish getting undressed, stripping down to his underwear and socks.

"When I told you, you were the love of my life, I meant it," he said, as he shoved my thighs apart and slid my underwear down my legs.

"How is that possible? We didn't see each other *that* often," I countered, stripping out of my shirt and bra. "Based on what you're telling me, I find it hard to believe our coming together as husband and wife was a coincidence."

"It wasn't…our fathers made a pact to marry us before we were born."

I bolted upright, practically knocking Ethan aside. "What?"

"I knew it would freak you out," he said, shaking his head.

"Of course it freaks me out. Eugene will never stop trying to control my life!" I ranted.

"It wasn't like that," Ethan said.

"Oh please do explain," I retorted.

Ethan sighed.

"They made a pact when they were in the Philippines, scouting land."

"Eugene told me about the trip to the Philippines, and how they were attacked by rebels... but I didn't know the details. He's not the most talkative man."

"After the rebels ambushed our fathers, they sent letters back to the States, demanding a ransom. Luckily, your father had been to Vietnam, and knew how to survive in the jungle. He eventually escaped, but came back for my father while the rebels were out looking for him. They hid in the jungle for two days, where they bonded, like brothers. In gratitude for saving my father's life, my father offered his first son in marriage to Eugene's soon-to-be born daughter. He agreed, but ultimately didn't take the pact seriously. After returning to the city, where they were safe, they went home, deciding not to develop property in the Philippines. But they kept in touch over the years, maintaining a strong friendship and business relationship in the process. Many years had passed before Eugene realized my father still expected their children to get married one day. An American education and wife would be good for his son. It would give us *face*.

So we visited from time to time, to see if you and I would get along. We didn't. We hated each other. So my father took me back home and told me to try harder. Next time, I hit you in the eye with a piece of chalk. It wasn't until your sixteenth birthday party that I'd taken notice of how beautiful you were. But I was tall, awkward, and lanky. My English was not only limited, but my accent was too thick. I knew you wouldn't like me."

"You have an accent now, and I like it…"

"Women love men with accents, I'm not so sure about sixteen year-old girls."

"I can't believe my father would do something like this…"

"What does it matter? It brought us together!" Ethan said.

"It's different for Americans, I guess. People rarely have arranged marriages in China anymore, but on the other hand, it's not usual either. Your father wanted to protect you, so he kept it a secret. He knew you wouldn't take it well…and eventually refused to arrange the marriage when you went away to college.

"I waited, hoping he would change his mind. But he didn't. So I used Byron Energy to force your father's hand, eventually repaying him the stock as a dowry after the wedding."

"You own Byron Energy stock?" I asked, too stunned to believe what Ethan was telling me.

"Millions of shares," he said. "I bought them from individual stockholders until I had amassed enough that I was able to threaten to sell them to Hammond Industries if your father didn't comply, giving them a controlling share. What he doesn't know is Hammond Industries is a subsidiary of one of our sister companies. Victor Hammond is merely the face of the company. My father and I are behind it."

"Why are you telling me this, now? You nearly ruined my family!"

I was angry with Ethan about the lies and deception, but I still loved him...after all, he'd done it all for me. He'd also transferred the stock back to my father, just on his terms.

"I wanted you and meant to have you," he answered, a calculating expression in his eyes.

"I was just a pawn in your game."

"You were the woman I dreamt of marrying for the past fifteen years, and now I have you."

"It's a lot to take in...a lot of time, money, and effort wasted on *me*."

"It wasn't a waste. If I had to do it all over again, I would. Although, I'm starting to realize you would have given me a proper chance if I had tried to win you over the right way."

"You're so cocky! What makes you think I would?" I asked.

"Because you're still here, after everything I told you."

"I'm in China. I don't have anywhere else to go!"

"You're still naked," he observed.

"Because your apartment is hot."

The next day, one of Ethan's security guards escorted me around Shanghai as I shopped for clothes. Prices were cheaper in the States, so the only thing I bought was a bracelet before heading back to the apartment.

When I arrived, I was directed to Ethan's office by Chan, who told me in an official voice, that Ethan wanted to speak to me. I walked in, to find him sitting behind his desk with his legs crossed, staring ahead with a blank expression on his face. His eyes were cold... harder than I'd ever seen them.

I wondered what was wrong, why the men were standing around, hands on their waistbands like they were armed and about to attack.

"Have a seat, Elizabeth," Ethan said, directing me to a chair on the other side of his desk.

"What's wrong?" I asked, sensing something had gone awry since I left.

Ethan laid a manila folder before me and opened the cover. I looked down. It was the agreement authorizing construction with a contractor for work on the hotel."

"You have any idea what you have done?" Ethan barked.

"They were cheaper than the other contractors so I made an executive decision," I responded.

"And now we're all in danger," Ethan shot back. "They're gangsters. It's 6 million on paper, and an additional 7 million behind under the table. I told you not to make any moves without my authorization. We had to pull out of the deal and now they're suing us for breach of contract. The lawsuit alone will cost millions. Do you understand?"

"You can't be serious," I said, unable to hide my shock.

"The hotel is finished. I'm canceling AmeriAsia's contract with Byron Energy, effective immediately."

"Don't back out, we can fix this," I cried. "Eugene will know what to do."

"You should have listened to me and your father before it happened," Ethan snapped, pacing the room.

I'm sorry," I replied, unsure that there was anything left to say.

"How sorry are you?" he shot back, slamming another file before me.

I looked down, a hand lifting absently to cover my mouth as I reviewed the contents in utter shock. The pictures Danny had taken were on Ethan's desk.

The photos had been altered to make it look as though Danny and I had been intimate. None of them showing my face, or the distress I was in when the pictures were taken."

"I thought the photos were old until I saw the ring," Ethan said. "So not only did you fuck me over in business, but you have *ripped* my fucking heart out."

"It's not what you think," I muttered, tearing up, as I gazed into Ethan's cold black eyes.

"It's all here in black and white," Ethan ranted. "By the way, I know about the money you took out of our joint account. The money you gave to your lover. Efrayim followed you. He saw you go into the

Cherry-House Hotel with a briefcase in the middle of the night, only to come out empty-handed. I checked our account. Did you think you could hide what you'd done because you put the money back? You screwed him then hid in the guestroom," Ethan sneered in disgust.

"He was blackmailing me," I cried. "I didn't know what to do…"

"Don't have an affair! That sounds logical enough, doesn't it?"

"I did *not* have an affair!" I pleaded.

"So it was a one-off? I hope the sex was worth it…" he muttered, tossing the photos across the room.

One of Ethan's men scurried to gather them up, his eyes turned away as he lifted them from the floor.

"It's not like that," I exclaimed, frustrated that I couldn't get a word in edgewise.

"I told Danny about the green card. He recorded the conversation, and told me if I didn't get give him two hundred and fifty thousand dollars he would send it to immigration. I would get five years in jail and you would be deported. I tried to protect you and my father."

Ethan shut his eyes in frustration.

"You're a very adroit liar. I don't need a green card. I've been a permanent resident of the United

States for the past six years. It was just an excuse to win your hand."

I stared in awe at Ethan, tears swelling in my eyes.

"And you say I'm the liar?

Ethan shrugged.

"What do you want from me, Elizabeth? Just go. Your services are no longer needed," he said, waving me off. "Efrayim…please escort Miss Byron to the airport. Make sure she's on the next available flight out of China."

"Please don't do this," I pleaded, feeling like the air was being crushed from my lungs.

Efrayim approached from behind and grabbed my upper arm. I looked over my shoulder at his face. It was the man from the photos I'd taken in Paris. I looked back at Ethan again, as Chan took the other arm, lifting me out of the chair.

"Ethan, I'm pregnant…"

I hoped that would be enough to stop the men before they ushered me out of the door. That it would be enough to make him change his mind.

"Congratulations," Ethan smirked, his eyes raking over me. "Who's the father?"

"Business as Usual"

I laid my wedding ring on his desk, letting it wobble toward the edge. And with that, I was swept out of the room and dumped at the airport with a one-way ticket to California.

CHAPTER 8

"It's about time!" Claudia said as she opened the door of her cottage.

I pushed my luggage inside and wrapped my arms around her.

"Hey, you okay?" she asked, concern warming her eyes.

I shook my head, confirming her suspicions.

"He dumped me," I sobbed into her shoulder. "He left me at an airport in China, alone and pregnant."

"Whoa! What did you just say?"

Claudia dragged me over to the sofa, leaving my bags at the door.

"I can't go home. Too many memories there."

"I understand," she nodded. "You can stay here as long as you want."

"You sure? Maybe you should talk to Wayne."

"He moved out."

"What? I'm so sorry, Claudia. I've been so involved in my own affairs I never got back to you. What happened?"

"We're getting a divorce. I'll tell you about it, but I want to hear about Ethan first."

I gave Claudia the short version of the story. But when I told her about Danny, and how Ethan had kicked me out of his apartment, she was piping hot.

"If I had a gun I'd shoot both of those bastards in the ass. You report what Daniel did to the police. That was sexual assault! Doesn't matter if he touched you or not. He forced you to take those pictures. Ethan said he was a permanent resident so you can't get in trouble for immigration fraud."

"I know... I'll deal with Danny soon. I'm a little fragile right now, and I need to rest. I swear, Claudia, I'm done with men forever."

"You were humiliated and robbed trying to protect Ethan, however misguided that was. No offense, honey. How could he treat you like this? Hell, even I'm upset!" Claudia wiped a tear from her eye.

"Have you talked to your father?"

"Not yet."

"He's looking for you. Give him a call," she sniffed.

"I'll use my cell phone. I'm in hiding. I don't want anyone to know where I am."

"Your secret is safe with me," Claudia said, patting me on the shoulder. "I'll make some tea."

I called my father. He answered my call on the first ring like he was waiting to hear from me.

"You blew it kiddo. We lost the contract with AmeriAsia. I told you Ethan was in charge of the project. Why did you sign the contract without getting our input?"

"I wanted to show you I could do the job," I answered, honestly.

"And where did that get you?"

Daddy didn't even bother to ask how I was or how I was doing. Ethan would never tell him about us, but he had to know something was wrong. He couldn't be that unplugged?

"I'm sorry kid, but I have to let you go."

"What do you mean?"

"It means you're fired. You failed the company and the family and I can't let that slide."

"I sacrificed three years of my life to help the company and now you're firing me? You'd think my sacrifice would count for something…after all, you did get your stock back."

"That has nothing to do with it," Eugene said.

"It has everything to do with it. That's why you wanted me to marry him. Now that you got what you wanted, you could care less about what happens to the rest of us."

"I was trying to save your inheritance, Elizabeth."

"*My* inheritance?" I huffed. "That's rich! The only reason you married me off was so I could give you a grandson to inherit your vast empire. You had no intention of keeping me at the company. I'm sorry Dad, but it's over. You can take your job, Byron Energy, the Gold Dust, and your inheritance, and go to hell. I spent my life worrying that you would throw me away and disown me like you did my mother. I don't have to worry about that now… because I never want to see you again."

I hung up, wiping tears from my eyes. I'd been kicked in the gut one too many times this week and it was time to move away from the people who were hurting me. However, before I fully moved on, I needed to press charges against Daniel. And I needed to do it before he released the rest of the pictures to the public.

"Everything okay?" Claudia asked, carrying a pot of tea.

"He fired me."

The pot shook as she tried to keep it from crashing to the floor.

"This is terrible. He can't do that to you! What was Eugene thinking?"

"You're on a first name basis with my father?"

"Of course," Claudia answered, sitting down. "I practically run the man's life, but trust me, not even I could see this coming."

"Now…I am officially done with men, and that includes my father. It's just as well that I'm pregnant. I have everything I need to move on, including a baby."

"What about a job?"

"I have enough money. Money I earned on my own, without my father's help. I'll find a job when I need one."

It didn't take long for word to get out about my parting ways from the company and that the Gold Dust Las Vegas had been canceled, pending litigation issues with one of the contractors. The story had been circulated in national news reports. But that was the least of my concerns. Taking Claudia's advice, I walked into the police department and filed an assault complaint against Danny. I gave them the condensed version of the story, telling them how Danny recorded our conversation and used it to blackmail me, claiming he would have me thrown in jail, and my husband deported, if I didn't give him money. I then explained that my husband had been a permanent resident for the past six years. I also told them about the naked pictures, and the stolen wedding ring. It was enough to get him thrown in jail a few days later. They found my ring at a jeweler in Daniel's neighborhood and a few days later, the ring was returned. I had it appraised hoping to sell it so I could buy a new house for me and the baby. The beach house was huge, but was more space than I needed. And the property taxes were excessively high. I needed a new home. Despite Claudia's many assurances, I knew I'd overstayed my welcome. I'd lived there for more than a month and a half. I felt guilty, forcing her to keep secrets from my father, knowing he was out looking for me. I had to call the Feds twice, to assure them that I wasn't a missing person. I couldn't go to the condo in Chicago, either. My father bought it and I wanted nothing to do with it.

Besides, I liked living at Claudia's place. It was cozy. I spent my newfound free time watching daytime TV, a luxury I had never experienced before. Me and the baby ate ice cream and other junk foods…also a luxury. But my sleepy days and nights on Claudia's sofa soon came to an end, when a woman from a magazine in New York called one day. She said she was from "*Le New York Fashionista*", an upscale magazine headquartered in Paris.

.

"Hi, is this Elizabeth Yu?"

"Yes it is. May I ask whose calling?"

"Francesca from Le New York Fashionista. How are you dear?"

"I'm great," I said, wondering what she was calling about. Francesca didn't sound anything like a telemarketer.

"Rumor has it you were recently separated from your father's company."

"Well, it's hardly a rumor now," I said.

"We were talking to our Paris office about you recently, and wondered if you were interested in working for *Le New York Fashionista*…we need an interim president for our U.S. based company. We make more than enough money in advertisement, but too much is going out. We need to bring someone from the outside in to audit our expenditures."

"That sounds promising but…"

What would they think about the pregnancy? Could I really take on a full-time job knowing I would have to leave when the baby was born?

"This may seem a bit odd, but our Paris office adores you. You were on the pages of every magazine a few months ago when you were in Paris. You are quite the Fashionista. We'll sell magazines with you in it. But it's your brain we're interested in. Our shareholders are getting nervous about all of the money we're spending. It will calm them down if someone from the outside joined our team. Who better than a brilliant woman and a style icon like you?"

"I'm terribly flattered," I stammered. "You mentioned the position was on an interim basis, but for how long?"

"Only a few months. Long enough to whip us in shape. We reviewed your corporate profile, Elizabeth. The job is yours if you want it."

A week later, I was on a flight to New York to meet with executives about the transition. Just when I thought I was down on my luck, something wonderful happened. The magazine was exciting, the people were beautiful, and money flowed like champagne from advertisers vying to buy their way into our pages. I just had to stop the financial hemorrhaging the previous president had caused. I was grateful for the short term role at *Le New York Fashionista* because the position would end before I entered my third trimester. The job had also given me the opportunity to prove I could make it without my father. I was immensely proud. I also had a corner office!

"You should start a maternity line," Francesca said, observing my wardrobe, as I walked into the office one morning. "You look fabulous."

I shrugged her off.

"These old rags?"

Francesca rolled her eyes, smiling.

"Seriously, I didn't do anything special. I bought what I normally would wear, just in a larger size."

"What? A size zero?"

I laughed in her face. "I wish! I'm starting to need an elastic band in all of my pants."

"Oh the horror," Francesca cried, a mortified expression on her face. "But you are right, that belly of yours is really starting to pop out!"

"I'll try not to eat," I assured her.

Everyone at the company was stick thin. I felt like hippo these days.

I walked into my office and sat at my desk, shifting through files, wishing my life was as perfect as it looked to people like Francesca. But none of them saw the real me... the one hurting inside. The one who'd lost the man she loved over a misunderstanding. The one raising a baby alone. People at the magazine only saw the pretty woman in designer clothes temporarily occupying the president's office.

Throwing myself into work was the only way I knew how to cope. So I was the last person to leave the office that night. It was dark outside when I climbed into the elevator, hand resting on my belly. The kid kicked a lot these days. At more than four months pregnant, he was making his presence known. I had an ultrasound earlier that week, and knew I was having a boy. I was a little disappointed at first. I was hoping for a girl. But in the end, the baby's gender didn't matter to me at all. I just wanted a healthy baby.

I also made an appearance in court to extend the restraining order I had against Danny. I won a default temporary order after he missed his court appearance while he was in the hospital. Thankfully he didn't contest it.

The elevator came to a halt a few stories down, the motion of the abrupt stop making me dizzy. I closed my eyes and took a deep breath as a man dressed in dark clothing and a hat stumbled in. The elevator started moving again, when he suddenly

E. Hughes

pressed a button causing it to stop. I looked up, ready to rip his head off.

"Are you out of your freaking mind? What in the hell do you think you're doing?"

Elevators made me nervous.

The man lifted the brim of his hat from over his face and looked up.

"I figure this was the only way I could get you to talk to me," he said.

I took a deep breath and pressed a button, starting the elevator again. I glared at the numbers blinking overhead while Ethan stared at the side of my face, as the elevator swiftly carried us to the bottom floor. Seeing him again hurt so much. Why couldn't he stay away?

"I miss you," he said, as I strolled out of the building into noisy Manhattan traffic without so much as a look back.

I hailed the first cab I saw and jumped in, praying he wouldn't follow me. It had taken months to get over what happened between us. And now he was back. Obviously I hadn't been punished enough. Ethan called my cell phone, but I refused to take his calls. He even left voice messages… but I deleted them unheard and had my number changed. I even had my cat Roger moved from the beach house to my apartment in New York, shortly after putting the

183

house up for sale. Despite the shaky economy, the house sold after only a few weeks on the market. I'd been a ghost for months. How did he find me?

The cab parked in front of the two story brownstone I lived in fifteen minutes later, to my relief. I had to use the bathroom. The baby, I was told, had found a place on my bladder. He was probably using it as a pillow.

I hurried up the stairs of my apartment building and stuck my key in the door, eager to get inside to use the bathroom. That's when I heard a vehicle parking in front of the house as the cab sped away. I looked over my shoulder at the dark blue Maybach and cursed. I opened the door to my loft apartment and rushed inside, slamming the door behind me. The doorbell rang a few minutes later.

I opened the door to find Ethan standing on my porch. I tried not to notice how good he looked.

"You found me. Happy now? Have your lawyer serve my divorce papers here, and not at my office, thank you. As you may well already know, I prefer to keep my private life, private."

"How could I forget?" he answered, eyeballing my perfectly made up face.

I folded both of my arms across my chest and glared.

"How did you find me?"

Ethan gave me an envelope and gestured for me to open it. My heart thundered in my chest as I slowly peeked inside, expecting divorce papers. Instead, I found a check for an obscene amount of money.

"What is this?" I demanded.

"A check for the beach house. That's how I found you. I got your address from your real estate agent."

"*You're* the buyer?"

"I bought it for us."

I took the check out and ripped it, scraps of paper falling between us to the floor.

"You can't buy your way out of this one, Ethan."

"I wouldn't try."

"Good. Now please leave."

He pressed a hand against the door as I tried to close it.

"How's the baby?" he asked, voice taking a serious tone.

"The baby's fine," I replied, giving him no more than that.

"Have you had an ultrasound?"

"Yes."

"What are we having?"

185

I rolled my eyes.

"As I stated before, I prefer to keep my private life private. And that includes my pregnancy."

"I have a right to know," Ethan pressed, stepping into the frame of my door.

"You're not the father, *remember*?"

Ethan's smile was faint. "I was hoping you would let that one slide."

"Not even if your life depended on it."

"Fair enough... What if I asked you to take me back? I miss you, Elizabeth. I wish we could get past what happened between us."

"You *kicked* me out of your country."

"Admittedly, I was wrong for that."

"You left me at an airport, alone and pregnant."

"I have no excuse," he said, looking down.

"You hurt me."

"I will never do it again."

"I'm sorry, but that's not enough. Why come back? Don't you realize how much you're hurting me just being here? I finally got my life in order and you can't stand it."

"I miss you, is that so wrong?"

"Right, because your feelings are the only ones that matter."

"After I saw the pictures of you and Daniel I flew into a jealous rage. I saw my naked wife with

186

another man. There was no reasoning with me. As far as I was concerned, you were having an affair. I now know I was wrong."

"Is that supposed to make me feel better?" I answered coldly.

"No. In fact, it only makes me feel worse. Especially after seeing the video, the way he treated you...when you told him you loved me."

I shrugged. "That was months ago."

You allowed him to humiliate you, in order to protect me... I don't need your protection, Elizabeth. I'm your husband. I'm supposed to take care of you..."

I tried to keep my tears in check as memories of that horrible night came flooding back.

"I'm sorry for rehashing the story. But you deserve to know the truth."

"There's more?"

Ethan nodded. "The idiot actually kept the footage, thinking he could blackmail you again. We paid him a visit a few days after you left. I wanted to deal with him personally."

"What did you do to him?" I asked, surprised by the revelation.

"We gave him a haircut. Needless to say, your ex-boyfriend had to spend some time in the hospital when I was done with him. We also confiscated the material, including the videotape, to keep him from using it against you. When I saw the footage, what you tried to do for me and your father, I tried to find you, I tried to apologize, but it was too late."

"I accept your apology, but unfortunately, it's not enough."

I moved to close the door in his face, but he stuck his foot inside.

"I'll prove how much I love you," Ethan declared, stripping out of his jacket.

He rolled up the sleeves of his button-down shirt then ran downstairs to the Maybach, where his bodyguards stood waiting for him. He then took his watch off and gave it to Chan before walking down the middle of the street until he was so far, we could barely see him.

"What is he doing?" I asked the guys.

Chan and Michael stared down the road in awe, as Ethan dropped to his knees.

"Kowtowing," Chan answered.

"Why?" I asked, completely confused.

Michael shrugged. "He's humiliating himself to earn your forgiveness. Some guys do it when their wives are mad at them. Usually when they cheat."

"Face is very important in Chinese culture," Chan continued. "This could be very embarrassing for him."

I shook my head, watching in horror as Ethan bowed all the way up the street, his forehead tapping the pavement, as he crawled forward.

I climbed down the stairs, and walked as fast as my belly allowed, as I hurried down the road to stop him. When he looked up, the middle of his forehead was bruised, his arms strong as they pushed against the pavement. I couldn't' bear to see him like this.

"What on earth do you think you're doing?"I shrieked.

"Begging your forgiveness," he said, tapping his head on the ground again. "I humiliated you, so why shouldn't I be humiliated? If I have to make a fool of myself to prove my love, then so be it. A man should never wrong his wife."

"Please stop…" I begged, covering my mouth with a hand.

"No."

Ethan bowed and continued down the road again until speckles of blood were left behind him on the pavement. Unfortunately, he was not only hurting himself, but he was embarrassing me. People came out onto the sidewalk and yelled for Ethan to get off the road before he injured himself, as cars swerved around him. Some of the bystanders even held cell phones and cameras, no doubt to upload video footage online of the fool kowtowing in the middle of the street!

"If you don't stop, I'll not only, never speak to you again, but I won't allow you to see the baby."

Ethan stopped dead in his tracks, but stayed on his knees.

"What are we having?" he asked.

"A boy."

"I was hoping for a girl," Ethan said. "So I can show her mother, how much I love them both."

"A healthy happy baby is good enough," I answered.

"Hopefully he won't end up in the middle of the street on his knees like his worthless father."

My heart softened, a little.

"You're not worthless, Ethan. You made a mistake and you hurt me in the process."

Ethan finally stood, turning to face me with blood on his bruised forehead. I winced as he drew toward me. .

"Thank you, for getting off of the ground," I said.

He was still handsome, even with a big purple splotch on his face.

"I'll never leave you again," Ethan said, drawing me into his arms, his eyes capturing mine.

He reached down, caressing my belly for the first time, the palm of his hand encompassing it as the baby kicked and fluttered. Then he finally kissed me on the lips.

"You still love me?" he asked, eyes swelling with tears.

"Love, is what got me in trouble in the first place," I answered.

Then I realized, he'd never actually heard me say it to *him*. It was no wonder why Ethan couldn't bring himself to trust me. Or for that matter, how I could trust him, after all of the deception and lies between us.

"I *do* love you," I confirmed. "Even against my better judgment, I want to take care of our family together. But I'm scared."

"I'll never hurt you again," he pleaded, desperately. "I love you, Elizabeth."

Ethan reached into his pocket, revealing the pink diamond wedding ring I left on his desk when he kicked me out of his office. He tried to slip it on my finger but I made a fist, preventing him from putting it on my hand. I wasn't letting him off easy. I didn't need another Eugene on my hands.

"We'll take it one step at a time," I answered, opening my palm against his chest.

Ethan tilted his face forward and kissed me.

"Now, let's put some ice on that stubborn head of yours," I said.
Ethan grabbed my hand and led me back to the apartment, and with a wave, the guys climbed back into the Maybach, driving away as we walked inside, leaving past hurt, lies, and betrayals outside on the doorstep.

The End.

Made in the USA
Charleston, SC
16 October 2012